November 2005

PENGUIN BOOKS

HOW WE ARE HUNGRY

Dave Eggers is the author of *A Heartbreaking Work of Staggering Genius* and *You Shall Know Our Velocity*. He is also the editor of America's finest literary journal, *McSweeney's*, and the founder of 826 Valencia, a non-profit educational centre/pirate supply store in San Francisco.

D0887875

HOW WE ARE HUNGRY

STORIES BY DAVE EGGERS

PENGUIN BOOKS

PENGUIN BOOKS

Published by the Penguin Group
Penguin Books Ltd, 80 Strand, London WC2R 0RL, England
Penguin Group (USA) Inc., 375 Hudson Street, New York, New York 10014, USA
Penguin Group (Canada), 90 Eglinton Avenue East, Suite 700, Toronto, Ontario, Canada M4P 2Y3
(a division of Pearson Penguin Canada Inc.)
Penguin Ireland, 25 St Stephen's Green, Dublin 2, Ireland (a division of Penguin Books Ltd)
Penguin Group (Australia), 250 Camberwell Road, Camberwell, Victoria 3124, Australia
(a division of Pearson Australia Group Pty Ltd)
Penguin Books India Pvt Ltd, 11 Community Centre, Panchsheel Park, New Delhi – 110 017, India
Penguin Group (NZ), cnr Airborne and Rosedale Roads, Albany,
Auckland 1310, New Zealand (a division of Pearson New Zealand Ltd)
Penguin Books (South Africa) (Pty) Ltd, 24 Sturdee Avenue, Rosebank 2196, South Africa

Penguin Books Ltd, Registered Offices: 80 Strand, London WC2R 0RL, England

www.penguin.com

First published in the United States of America by McSweeney's Books 2005
First published in Great Britain by Hamish Hamilton 2005
Published in Penguin Books 2005
1

Copyright © Dave Eggers, 2005
All rights reserved

The moral right of the author has been asserted

"The Only Meaning of the Oil-Wet Water" first appeared in *Zoetrope All-Story*. An earlier, shorter version
of "Climbing to the Window, Pretending to Dance" first appeared in the *New Yorker*, under the title
"Measuring the Jump." "Up the Mountain Coming Down Slowly" first appeared, in slightly altered form,
in *McSweeney's* Issue 10, also called *McSweeney's Mammoth Treasury of Thrilling Tales* – that edition
copublished by Vintage. "After I Was Thrown in the River and Before I Drowned" first appeared in
slightly different form in *Speaking with the Angel*, a collection of original fiction edited by Nick Hornby
and benefiting the London school called TreeHouse. "Your Mother and I" was published in *b2s04* and in a
chapbook put out by Downtown 4 Democracy. Many of the very short stories first appeared in the U.K.
Guardian. A different version of "Notes for a Story about a Man Who Would Not Die Alone" was first
published by *Ninth Letter*, the new magazine produced at the University of Illinois, which is the author's
alma mater, not to mention the proud and worthy recipient of two 2003 Nobel Prizes. The rest of the
stories were written for this collection and appear here for the first time.
Expansive thanks go to the editors who encouraged and improved these pieces – N.H., E.H., M.C., M.C.,
C.L., D.T., J.H., S.K., H.J., T.S., T.B., P.W., M.R., J.W., J.S., A.M., J.B., O.V.G., Z.J., A.V., J.T., L.D.
(light!), D.B., A.W., S.P., and to B.B., N.C., Y.H., D.K., H.M., A.L., A.V., D.L., and all at 826/McSwys.
Also to Bill, Hesham, Ashak, and all at the Webb-Waring Foundation/Kilimanjaro.
THIS BOOK IS FOR CHRIS.
VV: AOCWYGGL.

Net proceeds from the sales of this hardcover edition go to 826 Valencia, an educational nonprofit in
San Francisco, and to 826NYC/The Brooklyn Superhero Supply Co., an educational nonprofit in New York
City. For more information please visit www.826Valencia.org and www.826NYC.org.

Printed in England by Clays Ltd, St Ives plc

HOW WE ARE HUNGRY

ANOTHER

I'D GONE TO EGYPT, as a courier, easy. I gave the package to a guy at the airport and was finished and free by noon on the first day. It was a bad time to be in Cairo, unwise at that juncture, with the poor state of relations between our nation and the entire region, but I did it anyway because, at that point in my life, if there was a window at all, however small and discouraged, I would—

I'd been having trouble thinking, finishing things. Words like *anxiety* and *depression* seemed apt then, in that I wasn't interested in the things I was usually interested in, and couldn't finish a glass of milk without deliberation. But I didn't stop to ruminate or wallow. Diagnosis would have made it all less interesting.

I'd been a married man, twice; I'd been a man who turned forty among friends; I'd had pets, jobs in the foreign service, people working for me. Years after all that, somewhere in May, I found myself in Egypt, against the advice of my government, with mild diarrhea and alone.

There was a new heat there, dry and suffocating and unfamiliar to me. I'd lived only in humid places—Cincinnati, Hartford—where the people I knew felt sorry for each other. Surviving in the Egyptian heat was invigorating, though—living under that sun made me lighter and stronger, made of platinum. I'd dropped ten pounds in a few days but I felt good.

This was a few weeks after some terrorists had slaughtered seventy tourists at Luxor, and everyone was jittery. And I'd just been in New York, on the top of the Empire State Building, a few days after a guy opened fire there, killing one. I wasn't consciously following trouble around, but then what the hell was I doing—

On a Tuesday I was by the pyramids, walking, loving the dust, squinting; I'd just lost my second pair of sunglasses. The hawkers who work the Gizeh plateau—really some of the least charming charmers the world owns—were trying to sell me anything—little scarab toys, Cheops keychains, plastic sandals. They spoke twenty words of a dozen languages, and tried me with German, Spanish, Italian, English. I said no, feigned muteness, got in the habit of just saying "Finland!" to them all, sure that they didn't know any Finnish, until a man offered me a horseback ride, in American English, hooking his *r*'s obscenely. They really were clever bastards. I'd already gotten a brief and expensive camel ride, which was worthless, and though I'd never ridden a horse past an amble and hadn't really wanted to, I followed him on foot.

"Through the desert," he said, leading me past a silver tourist bus, Swiss seniors unloading. I followed him. "We go get horse. We ride to the Red Pyramid," he said. I followed. "You have your horse yourself," he said, answering my last unspoken question.

I knew the Red Pyramid had just been reopened, or was

about to be reopened, though I didn't know why they called it
Red. I wanted to ride on a horse through the desert. I wanted
to see if this man—slight, with brown teeth, wide-set eyes, a
cop mustache—would try to kill me. There were plenty of
Egyptians who would love to kill me, I was sure, and I was
ready to engage in any way with someone who wanted me
dead. I was alone and reckless and both passive and quick to
fury. It was a beautiful time, everything electric and hideous.
In Egypt I was noticed, I was yelled at by some and embraced
by others. One day I was given free sugarcane juice by a well-
dressed man who lived under a bridge and wanted to teach at
an American boarding school. I couldn't help him but he was
sure I could, talking to me loudly by the juice bar, outside, in
crowded Cairo, while others eyed me vacantly. I was a star, a
heathen, an enemy, a nothing.

At Gizeh I walked with the horse man—he had no smell—
away from the tourists and buses, and down from the plateau.
The hard sand went soft. We passed an ancient man in a cave
below ground, and I was told to pay him *baksheesh,* a tip,
because he was a "famous man" and the keeper of that cave.
I gave him a dollar. The first man and I continued walking, for
about a mile, and where the desert met a road he introduced
me to his partner, a fat man, bursting from a threadbare shirt,
who had two horses, both black, Arabian.

They helped me on the smaller of the two. The animal was
alive everywhere, restless, its hair marshy with sweat. I didn't
tell them that I'd only ridden once before, and that time at a
roadside Fourth of July fair, walking around a track, half-
drunk. I was trying to find dinosaur bones in Arizona—
I thought, briefly, that I was an archeologist. I still don't know
why I was made the way I am.

"Hesham," the horse man said, and jerked his thumb at his

sternum. I nodded.

I got on the small black horse and we left the fat man. Hesham and I trotted about five miles on the rural road, newly paved, passing farms while cabs shot past us, honking. Always the honking in Cairo!—the drivers steering with the left hand to be better able, with their right, to communicate every nuance of their feelings. My saddle was simple and small; I spent a good minute trying to figure out how it was attached to the horse and how I would be attached to it. Under it I could feel every bone and muscle and band of cartilage that bound the horse together. I stroked its neck apologetically and it shook my hand away. It loathed me.

When we turned from the road and crossed a narrow gorge, the desert spread out in front of us without end. I felt like a bastard for ever doubting that it was so grand and acquiescent. It looked like a shame to step on it, it was shaped so carefully, layer upon layer of velveteen.

On the horse's first steps onto sand, Hesham said: "Yes?" And I nodded.

With that he whipped my horse and bellowed to his own and we were at a gallop, in the Sahara, heading up a dune the size of a four-story building.

I'd never galloped before. I had no idea how to ride. My horse was flying; he seemed to like it. The last horse I'd been on had bitten me constantly. This one just thrust his head rhythmically at the future.

I slid to the back of the saddle and pulled myself forward again. I balled the reins into my hand and leaned down, getting closer to the animal's body. But something or everything was wrong. I was being struck from every angle. It was the most violence I'd experienced in years.

Hesham, seeing me struggle, slowed down. I was thankful.

The world went quiet. I regained my grip on the reins, repositioned myself on the saddle, and leaned forward. I patted the horse's neck and narrowly missed his teeth, which were now attempting to eat my fingers. I felt ready again. I would know more now. The start had been chaos because it was so sudden.

"Yes?" Hesham said.

I nodded. He struck my horse savagely and we bolted.

We made it over the first dune and the view was a conqueror's, oceans upon oceans, a million beveled edges. We flew down the dune and up the next. The horse didn't slow and the saddle was punishing my spine. Holy Christ it hurt. I wasn't in sync with the horse—I tried but neither the fat man nor the odorless one I was following had given me any direction and my spine was striking the saddle with enormous force, with terrible rhythm, and soon the pain was searing, molten. I was again and again being dropped on my ass, on marble, from a hundred feet—

I could barely speak enough to tell Hesham to slow down, to stop, to rest my spine. Something was being irrevocably damaged, I was sure. But there was no way to rest. I couldn't get a word out. I struggled for air, I tried to ride higher in the saddle, but couldn't stop because I had to show Hesham I was sturdy, unshrinking. He was glancing back at me periodically and when he did I squinted and smiled in the hardest way I could.

Soon he slowed again. We trotted for a few minutes. The pounding on my spine stopped. The pain subsided. I was so thankful. I took in as much air as I could.

"Yes?" Hesham said.

I nodded.

And he struck my horse again and we galloped.

The pain resumed, with more volume, subtleties, tendrils

reaching into new and unknown places—shooting through to my clavicles, armpits, neck. I was intrigued by the newness of the torment and would have studied it, enjoyed it in a way, but its sudden stabbing prevented me from drawing the necessary distance from it.

I needed to prove to this Egyptian lunatic that I could ride with him. That we were equal out here, that I could keep up and devour it, the agony. That I could be punished, that I expected the punishment and could withstand it, however long he wanted to give it to me. We could ride together across the Sahara even though we hated each other for a hundred good and untenable reasons. I was part of a continuum that went back thousands of years, nothing having changed. It almost made me laugh, so I rode as anyone might have ridden at any point in history, meaning that it was only him and me and the sand and a horse and saddle—I had nothing with me at all, was wearing a white button-down shirt and shorts and sandals—and Jesus, however disgusting we were, however wrong was the space between us, we were really soaring.

And I was watching. As the horse's hooves scratched the sand and the horse breathed and I breathed, as the mane whipped over my hands and the sand sprayed over my legs, spitting on my bare ankles, I was watching how the man moved with the horse. Somewhere, after twenty minutes more of continuous pounding, with the horse at full gallop, I learned. I had been letting the horse strike me, was trying to sit above the saddle, hoping my distance from it would diminish the impact each time, but there were ways to eliminate the pain altogether.

I learned. I moved with the horse and when I finally started moving with that damned horse, nodding forward, in agreement, in collusion, the pain was gone. I was riding that stupid and divine horse, attached to it, low, my head immersed in its mane, and I—

Hesham noticed I no longer struggled and we rode faster. We rode with the sun overhead. There was a wind in our faces, and I felt a part of every army the world had ever burdened. I loved the man I followed in the way you love only those you've wanted to kill. And when I was most full of love the pyramid emerged from the sand, a less perfect peak among the dunes.

At the Red Pyramid we went up its side, lifting ourselves onto each step, each great square stone almost five feet tall. At the entrance, fifty feet up, the man gestured me into a small black entranceway into the chamber at the pyramid's center. I followed him down and in, the passage steep, narrow, dark, dank, too small for anyone larger than ourselves. There was a rope that could be used to guide us to the bottom. I held it and descended; there were no steps. The smell was chalky and the air thick and difficult to draw. Ahead of me the man held a torch which carved a jagged light from the darkness.

At the bottom of the decline, we stood, turned into another hallway, now level, and soon ducked through a doorway and were inside a stone box. It was a completely unadorned room, with high ceilings and perfect geometry. Hesham waved his arms around the room with great proud flourishes. "Home of king," Hesham said, bringing his torch to one side of the room and revealing a long stone box, the tomb. The chamber was otherwise empty, devoid of any markings or jewels or masonry. Chambers like these had been raided endlessly over the centuries, and now all that remained was bare walls, smooth, with no sign of—

The air inside was heaving with dust and I felt we would

die if we stayed long. Would he try to kill me? Rob me? We were alone. For no reason at all I was without worry. We stared at each other in the room, neither of us truly impressed by the box we were in, though we both momentarily pretended at awe. I was disappointed, though I knew not to expect much inside these rooms. I didn't know how elaborate the space once was, but there was no evidence that it was ever anything but this, this sandy cube, and the fact of it saddened me. The exterior so magnificent, the core so crude. Hesham held the torch near his face and looked at me, though in the weak light I'm not sure he saw me at all.

He sighed loudly. His face moved through emotions: arrogance, boredom, annoyance. He was obligated to stay as long as I wanted to stay. I didn't want to stay at all, but I liked seeing him suffer, if even a small amount.

We climbed the steps again toward the crooked window of light where the pyramid drank the sky. It was dusk. Once outside and on the ground again, the man said, "There is another." I asked him its name. He said it was called the Bent Pyramid.

We were on our horses again.

"Yes?" he asked.

I nodded and he struck my horse with his open hand. I followed him though he was soon only a black wraith against a silver sky. Our horses were angry and breathed in hydraulic bursts. I realized now that Hesham was not doing this for whatever money I would give him. He hadn't bothered to negotiate for any of the trips after the Red Pyramid. What we were doing was something else, and each of us knew it. I was now sure he wouldn't kill me, and knew he had no plan, none more than I had.

An hour later we were at the Bent Pyramid, this one larger but less secure, and the light was gone. We climbed to its entrance and descended and once again found ourselves inside a sacred chamber, a room that had held a queen or pharaoh, though again the room was bare. The man and I stared at each other, breathing in the hard thick air, without any compassion for each other or anything.

What did you expect? his eyes asked me.

I wanted to know that I wouldn't die like a bug, I said.

Sorry, he said. These men died, were embalmed, and have been stolen. People sold them again and again. Their every effect, their bones, were traded for gold. You'll be no better off.

There's no reason to go inside these pyramids, I said.

No, not really, he said.

We learn nothing inside, I said.

Nothing, he said.

If these kings believed, why would they hide themselves in these plain boxes under these heavy stones?

Ah, but they didn't believe, he said.

That explains it, I said.

We left again and stood on the ground beneath the pyramid. It was dark as we mounted our horses. I swung my hand around, to encompass all the air.

"Good outside now," I said.

He smiled.

"There is another," the man said.

"I want to go," I said.

"Yes?"

I nodded and he struck my horse and we flew.

WHAT IT MEANS WHEN A CROWD IN A FARAWAY NATION TAKES A SOLDIER REPRESENTING YOUR OWN NATION, SHOOTS HIM, DRAGS HIM FROM HIS VEHICLE AND THEN MUTILATES HIM IN THE DUST

THERE IS A MAN who felt great trepidation. He felt anxiety and unease. These were feelings foreign to the man. He'd never felt this kind of untouchable ennui, but he had been feeling it for a year. He sometimes was simply walking around the house, unable to place exactly why he was tense. The day would be clear, sun above, everything good, but he would be pacing. He would sit down to read a book and then quickly get up, thinking there was a phone call he needed to make. Once at the phone, he would realize there was no phone call he needed to make, but there was something outside the window he needed to inspect. There was something in the yard that needed fixing. He needed to drive somewhere, he needed to take a quick run. The man had seen the picture that morning, in the newspaper. He saw the picture of the soldier's body, now on the ground under the truck. His uniform was tan, the soldier's was, and he lay on his back, his boots almost white in the midday sun, pointing up. Meanwhile, the man was sitting in his home, comfortable, wearing warm socks and drinking orange

17

juice from a smooth heavy glass, and was seeing the dead man in the color photograph. The picture caused him to gasp, alone in his home. He studied the photo, looking, he realized, for blood—where was the soldier shot? There was no blood visible. He turned the page, tried to move on, but soon returned to the picture and looked to see if any of the citizens of this faraway country were in the frame. They were not. The man stood up. He watched smoke billow rightward from a factory on the horizon. Why did he feel violated? He felt punched, robbed, raped. If a soldier was killed and mutilated in his own country, the man would not feel this kind of revulsion. He doesn't feel this way when he hears about trains colliding, or a family, in Missouri, drowning in their minivan in a December lake. But this, in another part of the world, this soldier dragged from his car, this soldier alone, this dead unbloody body in the dust under the truck—why does it set the man on edge, why does it feel so personal? The man at home feels this way too often now. He feels tunneled, wrapped, dessicated. His eyes feel the strain of trying for too long to see in the dark. The man is watching the smoke from the factory, and though there are many things he could do that day, he will do none of them.

THE ONLY MEANING
OF THE OIL-WET WATER

PILAR WAS NOT getting over divorce or infidelity or death. She was fleeing nothing. She flew to Costa Rica one day, on two planes, from Champaign, then Miami, because she had time off and Hand, her longtime friend, was there, or near enough. There is almost no sadness in this story.

Pilar: she is not Latin in any way she knows, but ever since she was very young she's heard from friends and strangers that her name is a Latin or Latin-sounding one. She is always embarrassed to admit, though she's admitted it a hundred times, that she's never looked up the provenance of her name, its meaning, or anything else about it. Her skin is the color of blond wood, easily tanning, and her hair is black, which reinforces the assumption of her Latinness, even though she's been told by her parents, always, that she's Irish and only Irish—maybe some Scottish, perhaps a jab of German. Though with her hair in a ponytail and with her long legs, very long for a woman not even five and a half feet tall, she resembles, more than anything, popular images of

Pocahontas. She always wanted to have some Native American blood in her, just as everyone does, because with that blood, she thought, stupidly, would come nobility, as would excuses to do things the wrong way, or not do them at all, to do anything she wanted. But instead she is Irish or possibly even Welsh but not in any tangible sense, and thus born without any sorrow in the lives of her recent ancestors, and so she had to smile gratefully and create good things from scratch or perhaps just save people from skin disease. Pilar was a doctor, a young one, a dermatologist. Her profession does not figure into this story.

PILAR WALKED: with her toes pointing northwest and northeast, like a dancer.

PILAR LAUGHED: in a throaty way, and loudly, while her eyes devoured.

PILAR KNEW: when something would happen, and when something would not.

Hand was in Granada, Nicaragua, for six months and was encouraging all visitors. He was working for Intel, doing something Pilar could never really grasp, even if she wanted to, which she didn't, because her brain, she believed, was meant to be filled with more colorful things. Intel had asserted itself in Central America and was rotating in young Spanish-speaking consultants like Hand for a year or two at a time. Pilar couldn't imagine what Hand would know that Nicaraguan Intel could need, but then again, this was the sort of arrangement he always landed—well-paying, low-commitment, impossible to explain. Pilar accepted Hand's invitation, but they couldn't agree on what the week would entail. Hand, sick of Nicaragua for the time being, wanted a week in Costa Rica, surfing and looking at women jogging across the flat wet sand. Pilar wanted to see Nicaragua, because everyone, it seemed, had seen Costa Rica, but no one she knew had set foot in Nicaragua. Nicaragua sounded dangerous; she liked the word. Nicaragua! It sounded like some kind of spider. There it goes, under the table—Nicaragua!

Hand got his way. They'd be surfing in Costa Rica, on the Pacific coast. But Pilar didn't mind. She would tell everyone she went to Nicaragua anyway.

In San Jose the humidity covered her with many gloved hands. She rented a car and immediately went the wrong direction, headed straight into the city's center when she wanted to do the opposite. It was easily ninety degrees and she was in the merchants' district, filled with cheap electronics and men selling things from white aluminum carts. Rental car agencies and banks and students. Clumps of pedestrians jogging through traffic. Office buildings of the sixties steel-and-glass Erector-set sort, flimsy and forgettable. The road was five lanes wide and was jammed but moving. San Jose looked like L.A. circa 1973, and she puttered through the city weirdly horny. The heat maybe. The volume of the sidewalks maybe. She watched women through her windshield and they watched her. She found an English-language station and on it Michael Jackson's "Rock with You" and she thought she would burst. She was happy, and she'd been for a few years able to recognize it, just dumb happiness, when it came, whatever its cause. When people asked how she was, she said Happy, and this made some people angry. There was traffic heading into town and she was moving, legs and arms and neck, with Michael, who she knew she'd like if she met him. She would understand him and they'd laugh and laugh about nothing, standing in his kitchen.

HAND HAD: loved three of Pilar's oldest friends, and she knew everything.

HAND WOULD: leave this world and everyone in it if given the chance to be in space for just a few minutes.

HAND CRIED: when he read about men falsely imprisoned, freed at age forty, and walking the streets without malice.

She found her way out of the city and drove straight west, through the tolls by the airport and then around the two-lane bends, hundreds of turns through the hill country, waiting behind so many trucks, everyone so slow. The countryside was neat and green and lush and everything was for sale. At the airport they had been selling real estate; at the car rental place, at every gas station, slick posters and handmade flyers of properties for the taking, beachfront or lowland—everywhere along the road, plots and properties available. The Costa Ricans were proud of what they'd created—the most sturdy, the most predictable, easily the most tourist-amenable nation in Central America—and now that it was ripe, they were bringing it all to market. The highway was tumored with SUVs and buses. Pilar had expected jalopies and wood-fenced fruit trucks, but they were rare. This country was singing with space and sky and bright smooth new cars with clean black tires. There was heat, but between the sun and the treetops were quick-moving clouds, and they dragged black shadows over the leaves.

LOW-FLYING, QUICK-MOVING CLOUDS: I haven't long to live.

TREETOPS, ROUNDED AND ROUGH: That's probably true.

LOW-FLYING, QUICK-MOVING CLOUDS: I won't even make it to the sea. I can already see where I'll end.

TREETOPS, ROUNDED AND ROUGH: I don't know what to tell you.

LOW-FLYING, QUICK-MOVING CLOUDS: But the thing is, I really love moving like this, though I know I won't even make it.

TREETOPS, ROUNDED AND ROUGH: There are advantages to flight.

LOW-FLYING, QUICK-MOVING CLOUDS: But thought is its unfitting companion.

Pilar was meeting Hand at Playa Alta, because there, Hand said, the waves were forgiving and not too big, the water warm, and the beach almost empty. Even when it's crowded it looks empty, this beach, he said. A big flat playa, he said, and she cringed, because Hand, she knew, would say *playa* when he meant beach, if that beach was located in a Spanish-speaking country. She loved him. He was ludicrous.

There is no way or reason to be subtle about why Pilar was in Costa Rica. At thirty-one she was still unmarried and Hand was one of her few old friends also still unmarried, and the only attractive old friend she'd never slept with. So she knew, when she hung up the phone with Hand five weeks prior, that she would sleep with him in Alta, and she knew it on the plane and on the drive to the coast.

Was she in any way saddened by the predictability of the outcome? Was it unromantic? She decided that it was not. Sex and things like sex—things people pretend they regret—weren't about a decision made in a heated moment. The decision is made when you leave the house, when you get on a plane, when you dial a number.

She would arrive and hope that he still looked the way she

liked him to look—lean, bigmouthed, clean. They would spend the first day pretending to be friends only, barely touching arms. The second night they would drink at dinner, and drink after that, amid shirtless and dreadlocked surfers, and then would sleep together in a tentative and civilized way. That much was assured, because Pilar had done this kind of thing before—with Mark in Toronto, with Angela in San Diego—and there was never variation in the setup; only the aftermath was alterable. Afterward, with Hand, there could be very little change in their affection and respect for each other: she was too careful, and he too loosely strung. Afterward, with Mark, she'd had to tolerate his frequent references to their weekend, both the almost-funny—"I saw you naked!"—and those helping him achieve a personal sort of release—"What were you wearing that weekend? Tell me again. Wait, hold on..."—but again, with Hand, she knew it would be mild, perhaps even forgotten, if it didn't grow into something else. But would they want to continue having sex? That's the simple and only question. And that depended on so many things: Would he do something strange with his tongue? Was his naked body odd in any disastrous way? Was he awkward-moving when nude? Would he cry (Mark) or become callous (Angela)? His legs might be too thin or pale, or his penis purple, or too narrow, his mouth too—

This story is not about Pilar and Hand falling in love.

Once close to Alta, the road devolved from two lanes paved to one lane dusty and everywhere potholed. The cars each way weaved and ducked, passengers inside with their hands braced against the roof. It was ten miles of this, and it felt like hours before the trees and farms gave way to the shanties and shops

that announced Alta. A combination juice bar and art gallery
called Forget It, Sue. Then a recycling center. More plots for
sale. The place was still raw, the road still dust. Barefoot boys
on bikes and mopeds outsped the cars, better navigating the
road's holes, while women let groceries in blue-striped plastic
bags pull their arms earthward. Just past a Best Western and on
the right side of the road, a thin line of trees hid the beach,
wide and flat, rippling into a delta berthing small boats of rot-
ting wood.

The hotel where they'd agreed to meet was called the
Shangri La, above the main strip, nameless. The town titled
none of its streets, but there was a primary artery, the length of
three city blocks, with most of the town's shops and restaurants attached. The Shangri La, on the hill, was white, and
shone like a monument against a teal blue sky. It overhung a
small garden full of iguanas, snakes, and mice, its deck jutting
its strong chin toward the ocean.

The owner, a fit and sunburned German named Hans, gave
Pilar keys and directions to the room, No. 5, and while walking up the steps and then along the deck, past the pool, with
a preposterous view of the big ridiculous Pacific to her left, the
sun teetering above, the waves blithely carrying surfers in, she
actually had the feeling, momentarily, that this was not, actually, her doing this, that in fact she was still in Chicago, or even
Wisconsin, and was imagining this—that she was just inhabiting a daydream concocted during, say, a dimly lit afternoon
salad-bar lunch at Wendy's. It really seemed more plausible
than the reality of her in this moment, actually walking barefoot around a pool shaped like a curling kitten, bordered in
hand-painted tiles of orange and blue, now stepping over two
teak-brown surfers on straw mats, on her way to a room, down
a long white hallway with geckos scampering on the ceiling

above, in a hillside seaside hotel in Costa Rica, which holds
Hand, whom she'd known for seventeen years, who was still
alive, and not only still alive, but *here*.

Pilar was worried that her back was oversoaked from the drive,
that Hand would feel her moisture and be appalled. But when
she opened the door and they grabbed each other and hugged,
he was just as wet as she was. He smelled like pineapple and
sweat. His chin was hot on her shoulder, his hair damp.

"No air conditioning here," he said. He said it in a gut-
tural Spanish accent. Pilar hoped he would stop.

"Oh," she said.

"Jesss, eeet eeez veddy hot here, jess," he said, and then
sighed, giving up.

The room was high-ceilinged and open, with a kitchen, a
breakfast nook, a bedroom a few steps up. A fan spun overhead, its pull string ticking with every two or three turns. The
deck overlooked the pool and the town and then the ocean.
She couldn't believe it all.

"This is crazy," she said.

"I know," he said, now speaking like he normally spoke.
She had known him since seventh grade.

The floor was tile. The whole place was tile. She had come
to expect carpeting in hotels.

"That's pretty normal down here, the tile," Hand said.
"Anywhere south of Texas is like that."

There was a plunger in the corner of the room, with a
handle that looked precisely like a dildo. She made a note to
joke about it later. Hand was standing in the corner. A gust
jumped through the open window and jumbled a chime over
the doorway.

She stepped over to Hand and slipped her arms around his waist and smelled his smell. She closed her eyes and pictured her old kitchen and the wallpaper there, a pattern of Disney dwarves bubbled from heat and humidity.

They left her things in the room and bobbed down the white stone steps. Outside, in the sherbet light that soon enough, with a shrug, would relinquish the day to night, there were horses. Four, just downhill from the hotel: one standing still in the road, two sitting nearby in the long gray-green roadside grass, the fourth one, white (the others were black), standing by the hotel's straight hedge, just west of the hotel's cherry door. Pilar and Hand looked around for the owners of the horses. They were shod but had no saddles, no bridles. Four horses, all gaunt, alone. Every horse stared at Pilar and Hand, two people from Wisconsin.

"I almost forgot you were coming," Hand said.

They were standing and talking while the horses watched.

"What does that mean?" Pilar said. She was scratching the top of her head with one finger, in a circular motion.

"I don't know." He stumbled for a minute, backtracking, explaining that he'd been looking forward to her coming, but that in the past twenty-four hours he'd spaced her arrival.

"You forgot it was today, or forgot completely?" she asked.

"Your hair is dark," he said.

"It was winter where I was. You're not going to answer."

"Did it used to be so dark?"

"I don't know. Didn't it?"

They walked by the horses; the horses watched with mild interest. Pilar didn't know what to expect from the horses. There was nothing remarkable about their appearance, but they gave her a chill and she wasn't sure why. She had rarely seen horses unaccompanied or unfenced and they looked huge and sinewy and tightly wound. She was enchanted by them, the novelty of having them so close to their hotel, but at the same time she wanted them gone. The size of their eyes implied a wide but focused intelligence, and she imagined that they would take the first opportunity to break into their room and kill them both.

"There's a woman here who runs on the beach every night," Hand said.

Pilar waited for something else from Hand about the woman, or the running—some point to the story. Nothing came. He looked at her, then down.

"There are some rocks near shore that you have to watch for when you swim," he said. "You want to swim now?"

Pilar didn't. She wanted to eat.

The dirt road was barnacled with small rocks, and huge rocks, and where it was not it was dusty and uneven. It was not a long walk to the beach, but it was too long. After thousands of miles of travel to reach water, even this, a five-minute stroll, felt cruel. The beach, once they ducked under a tangle of trees, was wide and flat; the tide was out. A woman jogged by the shore as her dog ran near her, jumping suddenly, as if jerked upward like a dog-marionette. But otherwise the place was empty, which was good.

"Is that the woman?" Pilar asked.

"I think so," Hand said.

"Are there other women who run on the beach at night?"

"I don't know. But it's dark."

Pilar wanted to cut stomachs open with glass.

*   *   *

Hand was tall enough, and built well, with flat strong pec-
torals and arms that were toned and brown. He'd been a swim-
mer in high school. But he also had a look of country madness
that everyone who knew him noted. It wasn't there all the
time—just when a subject had grabbed hold of his mind and
he was trying but failing, like Lassie and the well, to communicate its urgency. His was a nimble mind, sleeping shallowly
when sleeping at all—but there was a raggedness to his brain
that contrasted strongly with his attention to what he thought
were facts and numbers of great import. Handsome in a way
that sometimes looked bland, but there was character there—
a faint cleft in his chin, earlobes that drooped though had never
been pierced, some gray lines in his blond hair—that gave him
advantages and he knew it. The sideburns had come and gone
and now were back, and this was a mistake.

He had traveled widely in the past few years, since a trip
with a mutual friend of theirs, now dead, had brought him
halfway around the world in a week.

They shuffled down the main strip looking for dinner.
There was a tiny bodega selling *Miami Herald*s from the previ-
ous Friday. Some small homes. A shop offering only towels,
most featuring birds and monkeys. They found a restaurant
with Christmas lights strung from the roof, full of American
teenagers, all of them large, the boys bigger than the girls, huge
T-shirts draped over their fleshy chests. Pilar and Hand sat
down and in response a cat, gray with luxuriant hair, scooted
from their feet and onto the tin roof.

The waitress came. She said *Buenos nochas*. They said *Buenos
nochas* back. Hand said something in Spanish that made the
waitress laugh loudly. As she was laughing, Hand spoke again,
in Spanish, and the waitress laughed more. She leaned against
the table for a second with her hand. She looked at Pilar; she

was having a great time. Pilar had no idea what was happening. What had Hand said? Hand was a riot.

"What did you say to her?" Pilar asked, after she left.

"Who?"

"The waitress. What was so funny?"

"Nothing, really."

"You were killing her. What did you say?"

Hand wouldn't explain.

They ate dinner, chicken and rice, and wiped their mouths with the tiny triangular blue napkins provided. The cat returned and rubbed against Hand's shin, back and forth and again, in a way that began to seem inappropriate.

UNSUNG SONG TO HAND: There are things about you / Like your wide waist, which repel / me, but your lips, smiling / shake me, and your brown shoulders / pick me a few inches off the ground / I want to slap you across the face in the loudest way. CHORUS: I want to jump on your back and ride you like a mule / I want to jump on your back and ride you like a mule / I want to jump on your back and ride you like a mule. SECOND VERSE: You're someone who would lead almost any small nation / if you wanted to, but you don't / because half of you is odd / but still you have the charm of a leading / man, of an actor who was first a carpenter / someone who still plays lacrosse on the weekends / with the friends he's always had / I think your lips are too thin / your eyes too closely set / our children might be ugly / but you are a man, and there are so few men in the world. CHORUS: I want to jump on your back and ride you like a mule / I want to jump on your back and ride you like a mule / I want to jump on your back and ride you like a mule.

After they'd eaten but before they left the table, Hand said, "I think I want to make sausages."

Pilar pretended to be watching the cat on the tin roof.

"There are small machines you can buy that make sausage," he continued. "You buy the casings and then you stick the meats you want in there. Beef, pork, fat, spices. You ever made a sausage?"

Pilar shook her head. Hand fixed her with his look, brilliant and insane and grabbing.

"There are a lot of things like that, things you can just learn how to make. Like pretzels. Or doors. Regular people can learn how to make those things. Pillows. My mom started making pillows last year. She's made about eighty so far."

They walked back through the strip. Americans and Canadians and Swiss crisscrossed the street; some stood and watched the TVs positioned above the open-air bars, fuzzy college basketball happening, though soundlessly. Sunburned couples in white cotton fondled baskets in the souvenir shops. Surfers waited on benches for one of the two pay phones. Twelve-year-old locals sped by on ATVs, three on each bike, huge white smiles.

She counted the reasons she should sleep with Hand: because she was curious about sleeping with him, curious to see him naked; because she loved him; because sleeping with him would be a natural and good extension of her filial love for him; because there existed the possibility that it would be so good that they would change their ideas of each other and then think of themselves as a pair; because to deny one's curiosity about things like this was small and timid, and she was neither and didn't ever want to be either; because he had really wonderful arms, triceps that made her jangly in her ribs and tightened her chest; because she was not very attracted to him when away from him—she'd never thought of him while in the tub or flat on her bed—but in his presence she didn't want to walk or eat, she wanted to be nude with him, under a dirty sheet in a borrowed house. She wanted to hold his shoulders; she wanted to go snowshoeing with him; she wanted to go to funerals with him; she wanted him to be the father of her children, and also her own father, and brother; she wanted all this while also to be free; she wanted to sleep with other men and come home and tell Hand about them. She wanted to live one life with Hand while living three others concurrently.

At the hotel, the horses: two were sitting in the grass, as if they'd been waiting, patiently but with pressing business, the white one glowing faintly, like a star on the ceiling of a child's bedroom. The third and fourth were standing on the road, by the hedge, their dark hair shining.

HORSES: It's never like we planned.

HORSES' SHADOWS ON DIRT ROAD: I wish I could do more.

HORSES: We want violence, so we can kick and tear the world in thirds.

HORSES' SHADOWS ON DIRT ROAD: I'm helpless to help you.

HORSES: All we need is the spark.

HORSES' SHADOWS ON DIRT ROAD: When it happens, tell me what to do.

"Jesus," said Pilar.

"Maybe they live here," said Hand.

The horses had no symbolic value.

Pilar wanted to describe, to Hand, how she felt, every twenty minutes or so, about being there with him. They were together in the room, which had a roof and was warm. They were alive, though neither of them could have predicted with certainty that at their age they would both be alive—people flew on airplanes and drove cars after so many drinks, and every time they were away from each other or their family or friends, it seemed very likely to be the last; it was more logical, in some ways, to die or disappear. She had not grown up—her parents stayed home always—thinking that people could go far away, repeatedly, all over the earth, starting and finishing lives elsewhere, and then see each other again.

She wanted to rub herself in bananas. She wanted to open umbrellas into the faces of cats, make them scurry and scream. How could she sleep with Hand in this room? If it would be the only time, she wanted mirrors everywhere, so she could remember it a dozen ways.

But it would not be this night because he hadn't kissed her on the forehead yet. But this would happen. Tomorrow one of them would find a reason to hug the other, and they would hold each other for too long, making sounds about how good it was to be here, and then he would pull away a few inches, to kiss her on the forehead. And the rest would come soon after. She pictured his penis flying across the room and into her, and then shooting in and out. His head on the wall, mounted.

Hand took the couch and Pilar took the bed and they slept to the pulse of crickets and, above, the overeager tick-ticking fan.

The morning arrived with applause and they made toast. In the sun the dirt road was white. All was white. As if Pilar's eyes had been scrubbed free of pigment.

In a dark shop built to simulate a thatched hut, they rented two surfboards and the woman, orange-haired, oval-faced and Australian, pointed them to the nearest path to the water, across the street and beyond the blond sand.

They carried the boards across the white dirt road and onto the path, the sand soft and ashy. Through thin twisted trees and past a tin-roofed house, the beach spread left and right, flat and hard, at low tide a brown-gray parking lot. Close to the water the hard sand was wet, reflecting a blue sky, wide and musical with huge white flat-bottomed clouds.

There were dozens of surfers out already, ten just in front of them, another ten a few hundred yards to the right. The waves were small, with children playing in the shallows. Rocks to the left, body boarders close to shore. Pilar rubbed lotion on Hand's back and he did hers. Look at him, she thought. His face is strong. What would a man do, she wondered, without a chin! The skin on his back was taut and smooth. His neck aquiline, if that were possible. There was, she felt, a world full of beautiful future leaders, each with a thousand fulfillable promises, in Hand's neck.

Pilar couldn't surf well. She could paddle. She could lie on a board and balance and lay her face on its smooth cool wet fiberglass surface and rest. She was good there. And when the waves came she could do a few things. She could get up. She could stand, turn a little (only to the right), and keep herself steady for a few seconds.

But everything closer to shore for her, this day, was more difficult. She worried if she was holding the board correctly. She worried if when she drew the rented board from the rack, she did so correctly. She wondered if she was supposed to carry the board with its slight concavity out, away from her hip, or toward it. She worried if she should attach the Velcro ankle strap, which was in turn attached to the board and prevents the board from flying away after surfer and board fail, while *in* the surf shop area, once she hit sand, or when her ankles were wet with water. She didn't know if the board, when not in use, should be set upon the sand bottom-fin up, or down. She was concerned that if she did any of these things wrong she would be laughed at or pointed at and removed.

So she watched. She watched when others rented their boards to see how they drew them from the rack. She watched to see how they held them, carried them, when they strapped on their ankle bungees. And she did as they did, even though, as often as not, they didn't know either. Everyone was an amateur, everyone pretending at grace—that's why they were renting boards and did not own them, and that's why they were surfing here, at Alta, where the waves were small and forgiving and the water was warm, like the inside of a plum.

GOD: I own you like I own the caves.

THE OCEAN: Not a chance. No comparison.

GOD: I made you. I could tame you.

THE OCEAN: At one time, maybe. But not now.

GOD: I will come to you, freeze you, break you.

THE OCEAN: I will spread myself like wings. I am a billion tiny feathers. You have no idea what's happened to me.

Pilar and Hand walked into the water, same temperature as the air, and Hand bent himself in half, dropping his face in the foam and coming up headsoaked. He pushed the hair back from his face and looked at Pilar and Pilar knew that some people, implausibly, look better wet.

"The water's so warm," she said.

"It's the greatest water I know," he said.

They paddled out past the breaks. The waves were not large but the process was more tiring than she had remembered. She was knocked back six times and by the time they were on flat water again she was exhausted, her triceps aching, shuffling their feet, children in museums.

Pilar and Hand were straddling their boards, watching the horizon for coming waves.

A good swell came, five feet high, and with two quick strong strokes Hand was up. Pilar watched him depart for the beach. From behind, it looked like he was riding a very fast escalator. Or a conveyor belt. A conveyor belt being chased by a wave. From behind she saw only the round of the wave's top, and this obscured Hand's lower half. She was watching and he was going and going. He had a nice longboard stance, standing straight up, knees only slightly bent, leaning back, his whole frame one perfect diagonal line.

Then he was back, paddling quickly, smiling. He settled next to her and sat up on his board.

"That was nice," he said.

"It looked nice," she said.

Pilar liked what he had done, but for the time being she was content to sit. Or even to lie down. She had been in this town for half a day, awake this morning for an hour, and was prepared to do more resting, even if it was here, on the water. She stretched out on the board, resting her cheek on its wet cool creamy white, the wax, sand-encrusted, rough on her face. The water came over the board gently and kissed her. It said *shuckashucka* and it kissed her. She could sleep here. She could probably live here, on this board, her shoulders burning. There was no difference between resting her face here and resting her face on her mother's stomach when she was younger, no difference between feeling her breasts flattened against the board and feeling these breasts flattened against the backs of men. She liked to sleep that way, with men on their stomachs and her breasts on their back. It never worked—she never actually fell asleep in this position, but she liked to try.

With one eye she could see Hand, still upright, scanning. To the right of the beach, to the far right, a mountain, the color of heather, lay like a broken body.

"Are you going to take one of these or what?" Hand asked before dunking his head into the sea, coming up again so good, a mannequin's perfect head soaked in cooking oil.

"Right. Sorry," she said.

"Do you need a push?"

"Ha. Yes. Ha."

She had to try. She sat up again. They waited, both straddling, watching the blue horizon for a bump.

A bump was on its way.

"Take this one," he said.

"I know," she said.

She turned the board and laid her chest on it and began paddling. Three strokes and she was at the same speed. She let up and allowed the wave to overtake her. The wave came with the crackle of crumpling paper. She and her board rose above the land, one foot, three feet, five. The water brought her into its curved glass and she paddled harder as it drew her up and sharpened itself under her. Then two more strong strokes, both arms at once, and she descended. She knew the descending was key. That if she was not fast enough or her timing was off, the wave would speed below her and she would watch it leave, very much like watching the shrinking back of a missed bus. But if she were fast, or pushed at the right time, she would go down into it, and her board would speed up quickly, become a car, and she would jump to her feet and the board would become solid like a girder of steel, cream-colored, smooth, and doublewide.

This wave she took. The board was strong, she jumped up, was standing and traveling toward shore—she had gotten on the bus. Beneath her was all bedlam, foam and noise, the rush of white pavement. She had one moment of rapture—up! standing! look at the sun, the mountains like a body reclining or broken—and then she knew she had work to do. The wave was crashing from her right and she knew she only had a second if she didn't try to turn left, to ride the break. If she made the turn she could go for a minute, a full minute maybe, just stand and stand and stand. She had seen people ride these longboards for minutes, just standing, walking up and back, strolling—the best surfers could join their hands behind their backs and stroll up and back, up and back, considering the issues of the day, so sturdy was a longboard on a good wave, they could set up a nice chair and a rug and sit in front of the fire—

She wanted to turn left, to follow the still-curved glass away from the mulching glass, and so she leaned back a little, she weighted her ankles into the board's left side, pushing its edge slightly—

It was done. The board was behind her, gone. She dove into the foam and was under. Her ears exploded with the sound of underwater. It was dark and all was violence. She shot up and surfaced in time to see the board, wanting to be free but attached to her ankle, rearing, bucking straight into the sky before it fell again and rested into the now-calm sea of blue-green gel.

But she'd gotten up. A good thing, a bad thing—the rest of the day would be an anticlimax. She'd have two or three more good chances at most, no matter how long they spent out here. She paddled through the foam and into the calm again, the sun drying her back almost instantly. Hand was straddling, his feet kicking the water, waiting for her.

This story is equally or more about surfing. People are no more interesting than waves and mountains.

In the afternoon, on the hard beach, with the wind snaking at them, hissing and sending sand into their sandwiches, Pilar and Hand squinted into the sun to see the water. They'd been in the ocean all day and now were watching it like actors would a play going on without them. The ocean didn't need them.

Hand started clapping.

"I'm gonna clap every two minutes for the rest of the day," he said.

There was a man out in the surf, wearing a cowboy hat.

"What do you do for that company again?" Pilar asked.

"I consult. I brainstorm. They like my brain."

"But why here again?"

"My Spanish. And I volunteered. Down here money goes a long way. We get paid American wages but the costs here are half of what they'd be anywhere else."

"Okay, but why Intel here at all, and not Korea or something?"

"We *are* in Korea. A big setup there."

"Did you just say 'we'?"

"No."

"You did!"

The cowboy surfer was riding a perfect wave, hooting.

Hand had forgotten to clap. Pilar debated whether she should note this, knowing that she might just be bringing on more clapping.

"You forgot to clap," she said.

"Listen. I have no problem with them as a company. They make chips. Chips are good. They're in Granada because the workforce is educated, in the city at least, and they're good workers. The infrastructure's good, airport's good, roads work, communications are fair, banks are sound, inflation's fine, con-veniences are decent, at least in Granada. And because here Intel avoids the unions on the floor and in trucking, all that. A lot of companies are leaving Puerto Rico, for one because the union activity is getting big down there. Same workforce, basically, as here, but no one sets up in this part of the world to get mixed up with unions."

Pilar couldn't decide if she found this interesting.

Hand, remembering himself, clapped for a full minute.

The horses were outside again, but were loitering down the road, in front of the bucket-blue house with the German woman, no relation to Hans from the hotel, watering her rock garden. One black horse was scratching at the road, nodding, as if counting.

"Looking for water," Hand said.

Pilar went back to their room and filled a bowl with water. She came back; Hand's face was skeptical. She walked toward the horse. It backed away and trotted up the hill. She held the water at stomach level, dejected.

Hand walked over to comfort her. But when his arms

were supposed to wrap around her shoulders, he knocked
the bowl from below, overturning it deliberately, soaking
her shirt.

"Oops," he said.

She slapped him hard across the mouth and the crisp flat
sound of it made her laugh in one great burst.

There were animals everywhere. Underfoot there was always
something moving—lizards, crickets, mice. There were iguanas.
They could see them scurrying through woodpiles and through
the forest. In the thin trees below their hotel they saw an iguana
being chased by a yellow truck plowing away the underbrush.

The woman at the mercado had dirty blond hair, like mar-
garine full of crumbs. Pilar and Hand bought ice cream from a
freezer in the market. They tore the thin shiny plastic and ate
the chocolate coating first, then the white cold ice cream. The
sun made it soft.

At night they jogged through the alley behind the neighbor-
ing hotel, El Jardín del Edén, and down the dark dirt road to
where the loosely strung Christmas lights smiled between
columns, and techno taunted from speakers hidden in the
armpits of trees. Most of the restaurants were still open, their
attached bars ill attended. At the end of the road, past the pay
phones and the surfers waiting patiently in line next to the
local women, toddlers at their feet, they stopped into the Earth
Bar, its half-heart-half-globe logo hung low over the open
doorway.

Inside, people holding drinks. Shirtless thin tan surfers
and white men, young, with black dreads, were barefoot or

wore sandals, always with woven bracelets, beaded necklaces. The women were more varied. Plenty of the surf-girl sort but also backpackers of the Scandinavian breed—white-blond hair and bikini tops, plastic digital watches, reckless sunburns.

Pilar and Hand stood hip to hip by the bumper-pool table and drank very cold Imperials. The first two went quick—they realized how hot it was and how thirsty they were. They took their third bottles onto the deck, facing the black ocean. The darkness was close and concrete. They talked about the babies their friends were having, about Pete and April and their triplets. The last time Hand had seen April and Pete, they'd left the kids with the fifteen-year-old babysitter and stayed out until 3 a.m., refusing to let go of the night. They'd come home to find the babysitter asleep in their closet, their shoes piled up on the side. One of the babies had a bruise on his back the size of a wallet.

"In the closet?" Pilar said, and Hand didn't say anything, or maybe he hadn't heard. The story was missing many details and it made Pilar angry. But the music was suddenly loud and they didn't say anything for a full minute. A dog ran in circles on the beach, chased by a smaller dog.

Hand pulled Pilar into his body and held her.

"It's good that you came," he said. She murmured her agreement. He kissed the top of her head.

In front of their hotel room there was an anteater.

"It's not an anteater," Hand said, crouching down. "It's a sloth."

"Sloths don't have noses like that," Pilar said, "long noses like that."

It wasn't moving, but from its side they could see it

breathing, the rise and fall of its coarse fur.

"They sometimes do," Hand said. "Down here they do. Look at his toes—they're three-toed, like—"

"You don't know what you're talking about."

Hand opened his mouth then closed it.

"Maybe it is an anteater," he said.

It was bleeding. From its long snout there was a viscous substance that connected to the tile hallway, a stream of blood and mucus.

Pilar brought a saucer of milk. The animal made no movement toward it.

"It's dying, isn't it?" she asked.

"I don't know. It doesn't look hurt anywhere. Just the blood coming out the snout."

They decided to leave the animal outside. There was no animal hospital in Alta, and there was nothing they could do for it inside.

"But how the hell did it get here?" Hand asked. "It can barely move. How'd it climb all these stairs? It must have started weeks ago. And why'd it stop at our door? This is too strange. There has to be a reason. We have to bring him inside."

So they brought him inside. Hand did it.

"Like lifting a very fat cat," he said.

Now the anteater was lying under a chair near the door. Pilar put the saucer of milk near it again, and added another saucer of water. The animal looked dead.

"If it dies tonight, it'll smell," Pilar said.

"It won't die," Hand said.

Hand sat on her bed and Pilar stood before him. For a moment, Hand continued to watch the anteater. Then he looked up, grabbed her shorts from the front and pulled her toward him. She sat on his lap and leaned into him, but when she wanted to put her mouth all over his, he spoke.

"It's resting. It came here to rest."

The only graffiti Pilar had ever found thought-provoking was the line she'd seen again and again in bathrooms: *Sex invented God*. Each time she saw those words, for hours afterward, it was the way she saw the world, as stupid as she felt about it. She loved her life, but the only transcendent experiences she'd had began with provocation of her skin.

The animal unmoving, Pilar and Hand were side to side, and kissing slowly. Pilar wanted to kiss him harder and push him onto his back and stand on his chest and dance, but she didn't, because now they couldn't talk and they were strangers. She continued to kiss him quietly as they lay on their sides, facing each other. They waited for judgment, they wondered if this was working, they hoped they would get excited.

"Hi," she said.

"Hey," he said. "We should leave the door open. In case he wants to leave."

Hand got up, opened the door a crack, and jumped back to the bed. Pilar swung her leg around him. She was above him, straddling, and from her vantage point Hand looked so far away, so old and dead. She leaned down and held his face in her hands. "This face," she said. It was like holding a rock painted gold.

They took their clothes off and she lay on top of him, placed her ear to his sternum, and the water inside him went shuckashucka and kissed her again and again.

* * *

Where had she been snorkeling before? Florida, near Pensacola—another place where everything was for sale. It had rained all day and she and her father had gone in anyway, with rented equipment and just a few hundred yards out.

They hadn't seen anything then, everything so murky there, close to the breaks. But this, here, is what one wanted from snorkeling. The coral was dull colored, and there were no schools of fish. Here the fish traveled alone, loud blue ones, and very orange ones, small, and there was one with black and white stripes from stem to stern, and red on the hull. There was an especially bright yellow one that wanted to join Pilar inside her mask. It followed her, almost perched on her nose.

They had paddled a shoddy two-person inflatable kayak out to an island in the bay, hoping to watch the sunset here, closer to it. They'd pulled the kayak onto the island, which was not, as expected, covered with sand, but was made of shells. All of its white—the island was white when seen from the beach—was shells. Millions, edges and distinctions worn irrelevant. Pilar and Hand broke a dozen of them with each step. The outermost Pacific-facing side of the island was settled by what seemed to be pelicans but weren't; they were more elegant than pelicans, and numbered about fifty. The surface was lavalike, but was more cartilaginous than that. It was the consistency and color of burned flesh.

From the kayak they retrieved the snorkeling things, putting their mouths on plastic mouthed by hundreds before. With the cold fins snug they fell in.

All the fish on the floor were being pushed and pulled by the tide. And though this was their home, it didn't look like they were the least bit accustomed to the underwater wind. They seemed baffled and cautious, like Californians driving cars through rain. Pilar's hands, propelling her forward, appeared in front of her mask, glowing in the sun, angelic. She was an angel, she thought. But what were these fish doing here, where they were pushed and pulled by this bastard tide? This was nowhere to live. But these bright fish, existing only to be looked at, or pushed around, or eaten. She thought of people she had known. She forced metaphors. The sun shot through the surface like God imagined it, in straight and fabulous rays. The water was full of fish she'd seen in pictures and pet stores.

Pilar and Hand had woken up facing opposite walls but their ankles entwined. They smiled at each other and he reached over and grabbed her nose, as if to pluck it off. She knew that they would continue to sleep together because the night before had been good, and nothing wrong had happened. It would be this way: at night they would brush their teeth and sit on the bed and pull their legs around and under the thin blanket. They would scoot toward each other, their hands searching like those of children pretending to be blind.

To Pilar's left came three small sharks, striped, built like jets. They were headed for her. She was calm and knew she could make it safely. She pointed her head toward the shore and with her flippers gave the sharks a flurry of waved good-byes, the fins like handkerchiefs in a breeze. Close to shore she stood in the warm shallows, feet slipping over the mossy rocks, and looked for Hand. He wasn't anywhere. She wanted him not to be attacked by sharks. She wanted to sit on him, on this island, facing the sunset—it was all the colors of a bloody wound.

But there was a man on the island. She hadn't seen him before. Or he'd just shown up, and Hand was not visible but the man, not far away, waved to her and stepped toward her. He was about forty, and wearing a small swimsuit and sun-glasses, neon-framed, reflective lenses. She jumped back into the water, not fearing the sharks. He followed her to the water and then screamed at her, slapping his chest.

On the way back to shore, after she recounted the episode and described the man—Hand had not seen him—Hand scolded her for wearing clothes that invited the attention of men in the town whom the two of them didn't know enough about and couldn't necessarily trust.

"I've always wondered what it would be like to be seen as prey," he said.

He went into great detail about what the men in the town had been doing when she'd been walking by. There was the guard in front of the bank, who carried a semiautomatic rifle and, according to Hand, looked Pilar up and down and inside out each time they went into the bank or passed by. How does she decide not to wear a bra? Hand wanted to know this. Not to alarm her, he said, but men covet certain women, women they see every day. So perhaps it would behoove her—he used this word—to do more to disinvite the gaze of these men.

She was speechless. She was furious and confused and ashamed and wanted to club him and kick him and jump on his head.

"I care about you, Pilar," he said. "Don't get pissed. And don't make that face."

Her lower teeth were jutting out, like a piranha's. She knew she did this. She was angry that it was now this way with them, and so soon: she was not free. She would be given advice, or whatever it was. They paddled and she focused on the broken hillside. She put Hand in a new category. He was *that.* This was this, and nothing more.

* * *

In the evenings the sun dropped through the ocean and the sky would darken quickly. Armadillos scurried below their deck, under the streetlamp, their shiny shells sniffling through the high grass. Under the bed where Pilar and Hand slept, platoons of ants circled around crumbs and moved them to the door, under, and on to parts unknown. Geckos squiggled up and down the wall above the screen door, heading to and from what appeared to be their home, in the beam in the center of the room. The dusty white light during the day never wavered. There were three or four clouds all week.

For a few days Pilar and Hand were married. They surfed and rested their boards fin-up on the hard sand, sat on the flat beach, ate round crackers and drank Fanta. They watched the water, eating nuts and cookies. After they finished eating they would nap, her head in his stomach, and in an hour they would paddle out again. They would stay in the water until the water became black, and then stay until the sun set into it and the black water was striped orange loosely.

At night the surfers roamed the streets barefoot but with hair fluffy from having been finally washed. Couples walked, leaning into each other while glancing at people they found more attractive. Or maybe not. There was no way to know what they were thinking.

Every night, after dinner, Pilar and Hand bought ice cream from a man who had been burned on half of his face. Burned or perhaps it was coming from below—his face had great growths on it, oval and coarse, like the ass of a boar. Usually the moon was yellow behind Vaseline. Sometimes there was hay on the street.

One night they went to see the huge migratory turtles huff ashore and lay their eggs, hundreds of eggs, all of them soft and slathered in gel. They stood behind one enormous one as it swept sand into its hole, sprinkling each group of eggs.

Some days they could hear people playing tennis, but they could not see the court, and even looked for it one day and could not find it. They watched a man painting a picture of the beach; he welcomed their watching and talking. He was from Philadelphia and had had a bad year, a litigious divorce and a friend dead, killed driving to Tahoe.

They slept together once sober and it was awkward—they were not lovers but friends playing Twister. They went back to their original plan the next night. They drank a bit, and then went to bed, just under the surface of consciousness, feeling no edges. Someone watching them from afar might ask: How did they speak to each other? The answer: With the warmth of very old friends, though they were not yet old. How did he touch her? Clumsily, for he was clumsy and she was critical. How did she kiss him? Desperately, pulling and pushing, like a woman trying to get to the bottom of a deep pool.

When they walked usually there were stones in their shoes, because the road was dotted with pebbles and their shoes were loose.

They were leaving Alta the next afternoon—Pilar for home and Hand for Granada and there were no future plans—so they rented boards early and were in the water by nine. It was an uncomplicated day.

Hand was out in the sea before her and she watched him until she was too hot to stay dry. She paddled past the breaks, which meant pushing through four full waves collapsing, like drunks, onto her. Each time she would have to either push the board's nose into the wave and hope she stayed on, or would preemptively surrender, diving off, waiting for the board to bungee away and come back to her. She had never been so tired.

Hand soon shot past her, on a bigger wave, one that would have crushed Pilar had she tried it. She watched him speed into the beach, looking like he was going faster than the wave. She noticed that people riding waves seem to be moving much faster than waves do when they're traveling without passengers. Hand had caught this one at the perfect moment and was riding it left, on and on, as it sped away and toward the estuary. It seemed endless. He waved to Pilar. She waved back. It's weird, Pilar thought, to wave to someone while they're standing on water. She maybe loved him.

She sat up again, watching the flat blue for growths.

If there were a question that needed to be answered in this story it would be not one but many, and would be these: How can a world allow all this? Allow these people to live so long? To travel all these miles south, to a place so different but still so comfortable, and in that place, meet again? To allow them to be naked together for the first time? What would their parents think? What would their friends think? Would anyone object? Who would plan for them? How many times in life can we make decisions that are important but will not hurt anyone? Are we obligated—maybe we are—to say yes to any choice when no one will be hurt? We use the word *hurt* when talking about things like this because when these things go wrong it can feel as if you were hit in the sternum by a huge animal that's run for miles just to strike you.

In two hours, she found two waves. Waves were something she cared about now. But she began to care more about seeing them than catching them, and more about catching them than riding them, and above all she wanted to simply stay out beyond the breaks. Because after each ride, the trip back, past the breaks, was too much.

Her arms seemed so thin, like narrow dowels being pushed through syrup. The ache at her shoulders brought her near tears. It wasn't right that it should be so hard, especially here. The waves would crash ahead of her and the tall strong foam would roll at her, and would then run over her. Knocked off the board, she would scrape the water off her face, spit, expel snot, jump back on the board, paddle twice, achieve maybe ten feet of progress out, and then get knocked over again. Her spirit was broken many times.

She closed her eyes. Opened them, closed them. She could end this world or allow it. This was a moment when a believer, a thoughtful believer, would think of God's work, and how good it was. The waves were perfect to the right and perfect to the left. Far away there were loud long hoots from the man in the cowboy hat, riding a long low slow breaker all the way in. Pilar thought of the man at her church group who taught everyone how to win at pinball. She thought of curved penises. For a while she was enchanted by those who proposed that God was in nature, was all around us, was the accumulated natural world. "God," they would suggest, "is in all living things. God is beauty, God is in the long grass and the foam finishing a waterfall." That sort of thing. She liked that idea, God being in things that she could see, because she liked seeing things and wanted to believe in these things that she loved looking at—loved the notion that it was all here and easily observable, with one's eyes being in some way the clergy, the connection between God and—

She saw Hand, almost at the estuary, finally end his ride, nimbly stepping off his board and into the water, as if descending from a chariot. He stood for a second, knee-deep, and adjusted his bathing suit. Then he doubled over again and dumped his head. Had his hair had gone dry during his ride? Incredible. He wouldn't be back for a while.

But a single contained God implied or insisted upon a hierarchy that she didn't accept. God gave way to a system of extremes, and implied choices, and choices required separations, divisions, subtle condemnations. She was not ready to choose one God, so there would not be this sort of god in Pilar's world, and thus the transcendental deity—

But then why God at all? The oil-wet water was not God. It was not the least bit spiritual. It was oil-wet water, and it felt perfect when Pilar put her hand into it, and it kissed her palm again and again, would never stop kissing her palm and why wasn't that enough?

Her board was pointing almost directly toward the now-dimming sun. The dimming sun made the water seem even more like oil, and where the sun did not highlight the water, the water was black. The sun was large and was more three-dimensional than usual. The water was black where the sun wasn't making it gold. The water was getting warmer and the surfers around her became with each passing minute more abstract, closer to silhouettes, moving in slow motion.

She sat up on the board, straddling it. She didn't want to surf. She wanted to sit here for a long time, the waves behind her, ridden by the vague black figures. She wanted only to sit and stare ahead and wait for more of the water to go golden.

When the sun fell and the water turned black she would ride the last wave in and sleep. She felt that she knew how her old age would feel. She would be too tired to move. She knew that if she rode in she would not be able to ride out again.

* * *

They left the town at dusk. The roped road was potholed completely, full of slow-driving tourists in SUVs, so careful with
their rentals, like elephants stepping gingerly around puddles.
Pilar and Hand passed and left them and drove away from a
dusk gaudy with purple. The road went from dirt to gravel to
finally pavement unpotholed, but remained two lanes, winding
back and forth over hills and down hills and always under a perfect canopy of trees with long fingers overhead laced.

When the night went black they realized their lights were
too bright. Passing cars thought their high beams were on, and
flashed them. They flashed them back, showing them their real
brights, and then, to retaliate, the cars would flash theirs
again. It happened a hundred times. They hated the implica-
tion of their thoughtlessness, and the strain on their eyes was
terrible, all the flashing, all that quick bright anger.

The night before, it was windy and restless outside, and Pilar
and Hand had recently fallen asleep and were still lying front
to back, Hand's knees behind Pilar's knees. There was a loud
thump. Hand sat up and when Pilar moved to investigate, he
gestured her to stay in bed. She did because she wanted to see
what he would do. Was she scared? She was. Hand had made her
convinced—more when she thought about it than when she
didn't—that the man from the bank would come, with his
gun, and kill Hand and then rape her.

Hand was at the front door of the room when Pilar looked
up and found the origin of the sound. It was a hole in the roof,
over the bed, where the skylight once was. The wind had
pulled the skylight off, and Pilar could see the clear black

night through the square in the ceiling. Hand came back to bed and they were friends in bed together, nude. Hand said he liked going to the door to look for invaders and Pilar said she was glad it was a hole in the roof.

ON WANTING TO HAVE
AT LEAST THREE WALLS UP
BEFORE SHE GETS HOME

HE IS BUILDING a small house in the backyard for when their baby is old enough to use it as a fort or clubhouse or getaway, and he wants to have three walls up before his wife gets home. She is at her mother's house because her mother has slipped on the ice—a skating party, Christmas-themed—and needs help with preparations for her holiday party, planned before the accident. It's snowing lightly and the air is cold enough to see. He is working on the small house with a new drill he's bought that day. It's a portable drill and he marvels at its efficiency. He wants to prove something to his wife, because he doesn't build things like this often, and she has implied that she likes it when he does build things, and when he goes biking or plays rugby in the men's league. She was impressed when he assembled a telescope, a birthday gift, in two hours, when the manual had said it would take four. So when she's gone during this day, and the air is gray and dense and the snow falls like ash, he works quickly, trying to get the foundation done. Once he's finished with the foundation, he decides that to impress her—and he wants to impress her in some way every day and wants always to want to impress her—he will need at least three walls up on the house by the time she gets home.

CLIMBING TO THE WINDOW,
PRETENDING TO DANCE

THREE HOURS on I-5 so far, straight as a tightrope, and every twenty minutes or so he sees one of those birds. Always near the roadside, on bent fenceposts or hopping in the gray flossy grass, they look like crows but with breasts a militant strain of orange. They come with an eerie regularity, ten already, and they are alone. <u>Fish</u>, approaching thirty and driving eighty, doesn't know what to call these birds. They are wretched birds.

It's a merciless drive from San Jose to Bakersfield—you'd think it was Iowa or Texas if you couldn't, faintly, sense the sea air coming over the western hills. Inland like this, it's hotter and more humid than Fish, who grew up in Illinois, wants California to be. Heat echoes off the road in liquid waves, cars heave with asthma, and Fish's penis is sticking to his thigh in a way that seems irrevocable. It's actually a decent drive for a while—all those velour hills by the dropping of a barn-red sun—but then the road just goes, moaning its way south, and it's so straight you want to kill it all and chop your god-damned head off.

Fish tells himself, audibly, not for the first time, that he would kill his cousin Adam if he had the chance and could get away with it. As children, he and Adam were made to think of each other as brothers, because their mothers were close and neither of them had a male sibling.

They looked nothing alike.

Adam was an only child, while Fish has a younger sister, Mary, married now and with two sets of twins, all of them freckled and insane—they jump on visitors like dogs. Adam lived in Aurora and Fish lived in Galena, so they saw each other only once a month and in the summers went on uneventful canoe trips in lower Wisconsin, passing in their quiet canoe groups of sharp-toothed kids, poor, wearing bandannas and white rope bracelets.

Fish is driving to see Adam—there goes another one of those black birds, with plumage like a chest exploding—because Adam has tried to kill himself again. This is his seventh attempt, and now Fish knows he should have flown. San Jose, he's almost sure, has a direct flight to Bakersfield, less than an hour in the air. Piss! Every time he finishes this drive he vows never again, and then two months later he's here, punching the window, back soaked, left arm sunburned, cursing himself.

Five hours at least, this drive, plenty of time to come up with a plan, something to say. He tries to concentrate on Adam but finds himself constantly adrift and onto other subjects, like food and war. Years ago he thought he could have an effect on Adam's life, but now he knows he's a spectator, a parent watching a child's sporting event, hands twisted into fists, unable to influence the outcome.

Fish passes a huge beef-processing plant, where a hundred thousand cows are kept so close they can't move their tails enough to swat flies. There is no earth visible below their doomed hides. He rolls up the window, the stench vile, punishing. Those stupid cows, he thinks, born to die, born to be eaten, born to walk in their own feces. Jesus! It smells fetid, bloody and sweet, like human innards, if you could open yourself up and bring it all to your nose and inhale.

Adam doesn't talk to his mom or to Fish's parents, and he's never had a job, none that Fish can recall, which in a way is impressive, how he's been able to get by for so many years without any sort of legitimate income. There are people who do this, who divert just enough energy and funds and goodwill from those close to them to exist without anyone taking much notice; it's like stealing cable, but on a larger scale. Fish has given Adam about twenty-two hundred dollars over the years, which he has used frugally—he is clever that way. He's clever in every way, really, even in surviving so many attempts on his own life. Maybe he's unkillable, Fish thinks, and he suddenly snorts out loud at the thought.

Fish's other cousin, Chuck, a tax lawyer in Charlotte with the face of a priest, rose-colored and surprised, says that Adam looks about forty now, though he's only twenty-eight. The drugs do that, Chuck says. Chuck should know.

Fish hasn't seen Adam in almost a year and now he's afraid to. If Adam looks old, it means Fish is old and they're both old, everyone's old, and— Damn, another one of those birds. There must be a name for those things.

 Adam's hope, Fish is sure, is to be the shape-shifting mystery spot in the life of his family and friends. The problem is that Fish has never had a fascination with people who try to kill themselves. Maybe if he took more of an interest in the concept, Adam wouldn't keep trying to prove how intriguing it is. With the resources they required of everyone around him, Adam's life and his attempts on it were a kind of vacuum, into which he pulled the good air around him, and everyone close to him—took their words and possibility for joy. And yet in most ways Adam is nowhere near as strange, for example, as the guy who delivers Fish's mail, a man named Kojo.

"Short for Kojak?" Fish asked when they met. It was a dusty day, windy, the sun like a planet of sand. The mailman laughed. He laughed for about ten minutes over that one. Fish was flattered, then he was scared. Kojo liked to laugh, laughing in a big, unconvincingly expansive way, but he didn't like to wear the postal pants. He always wore the shorts, no matter how cold it got.

He came into Fish's house once for a beer, and he drank with his mouth all around the bottle, as if fellating it. Then he unrolled his sleeve and showed Fish a skin graft he'd got—*just for the wack of it,* he said. "Took some skin from my lower back and put it on my arm." The pores in the new skin were smaller and the surface was smoother, less weathered. There are doctors, Kojo said, who'll do anything for the right money.

A week later Kojo brought Fish a collage, the kind junior-high girls assemble, with phrases cut from women's magazines—"Only Best Friends Know!" "Quiz: Are His Pals the Real Deal?"—pasted over pictures, cut from books, of Winnie the Pooh and Piglet flying kites together, walking through the woods at night, among the trees with muscular trunks.

Fish attracts these people. In high school there was an older guy, a senior when he was a sophomore, tall and bent backward. He had a huge, almost perfectly square head, and he wanted Fish to drive cross-country with him, though they'd talked only once, briefly, while they were watching the girls' swim team practice.

"I like butterfly," the guy had said. His name was either Brendan or Brandon or Stuart.

"Butterfly's good," Fish had said.

That had been their conversation, all of it, and two months later a breathless Brandon appeared, grinning, forehead wet with concentration, when Fish was walking out to soccer practice. "Don't say no, Fish. We're gonna head out and fuck this fucking school and drive to Florida. Fuck this fucking fuck!"

Fish, not wanting to say no, just said "Sorry," and followed the rest of the team over the hill, to the upper field, rectangular but sloping on every side, like a freshly filled grave.

When Kojo presented the collage to Fish, insisting that he open it there in the doorway, Fish didn't know what to say. He shook his head in a kind of awe, then thanked Kojo and made plans to see him three weeks hence—they'd have a beer at the end of the month, just *tear it up,* yeah—then, the next morning, Fish got himself a post-office box.

Fish is driving, slapping himself to stay alert, and he's counting, to be sure it's been seven times for Adam. One: the wrists (with an small saw on his thin, paper-white arms). Two: poison—he drank floor wax, first pouring it into a tall clear glass. Three: the gunshot to the stomach. Or the side of the stomach—the bullet grazed him and went through his window and into the Episcopal church next door. No one was killed or hurt, but Adam felt so bad about it that, four, he stabbed himself in the leg with a cleaver. Five: he tried bringing a hair dryer into the tub with him, but it was suicide-proof, apparently—it turned itself off, leaving Adam shivering, the water having gone cold while he'd got up the nerve. Six: what was six? A car driven into a tree? There was debate about whether that one had been intentional.

This time, two nights ago, Adam, half drunk—he was always impaired when he tried these things—jumped off a motel roof. At least that's what Chuck heard from the para-medic who found Adam, unconscious in the parking lot, splayed like a buck on the hood of a truck. It was about forty feet down, Chuck said.

Adam could have jumped into a dry gorge a few blocks from the motel and he would have died for sure—the dropoff there was about a hundred feet. Instead, he fell four stories, into the courtyard, broke his collarbone, cracked his left leg, bent his spine.

The road is quiet. I-5 is split, a narrow valley between the comers and the goers, so Fish, his brain marshy and his eyes glazed, can see only the cars that are heading in his own direc-tion. Fish likes to see the faces of people going the other way, to construct stories about them, wish them well or ill, but this is nothing, this drive—this is sorrow. It makes you want to freeze the world and shatter it with an ax.

This morning Fish's pillow was soaked and his blanket was halfway out the window; he woke up hearing machine guns and screams. Not unusual, but this time he was on the plane, not watching it. It hadn't taken off yet. There was something wrong, the air of the world had shrunk in on itself and then the men burst in. They pulled guns from a compartment and start-ed shooting, endlessly, from the front to back, everything mov-ing too slowly. Fish was in one of the last rows, listening to the shrieking, constant but undulating, and he was planning, clenching and unclenching his fists, looking around, between seats behind and in front of him, for a couple of people to come with him and help him end this. The fact that he was alive to hear the suffering meant that he was meant to stop it.

Through breakfast Fish was still operating under the blurry assumption the attack had been real, but CNN said nothing about it. Still, he was down, foggy, feeling remorse. He was crushing aluminum cans in the driveway, distracted, nerves shot, when Chuck called from Charlotte and described what Adam had done.

"I'm not going this time," Fish said.

"I can get there four days from now," Chuck said. "Do one day before I come. Make sure he's not paralyzed. Check that they have him in a real room and everything." Two years ago, after No. 3, Chuck arranged insurance for Adam, an expensive plan, and was frequently checking to make sure he was getting his money's worth.

Chuck doesn't know Adam as well as he pretends, and thus his benevolence can be less complicated than Fish's. He never shared a bedroom with Adam. He never found Adam's crusty tissues stuffed, like brains displayed in a jar, in a curvy blue bottle he'd won at a carnival. He never caught Adam rubbing down Mary's legs after track, his hands wrapped like tentacles around her calves.

Fish is driving a rental car. He called the place where they pick you up in a sedan wrapped in brown paper. He called at about noon and they said they'd send the car over at two. Between twelve and two, he waited in his house. He watched baseball on TV. He put in a videotape of him and his father running in a Chicago marathon. His dad was wearing the brace he wore during those years, and he has a mustache. When he sees the camera, he turns around and runs backward. Then Fish's mom drops the camera and the tape ends. Adam was no athlete. There was a game Fish played with him—it was

Adam's only good toy—where tiny metal football players move around on a field vibrating below them. It was a strange device, because you couldn't really control the little bastards—you just watched as the field sent them jerking around, crowding together or falling alone.

Fish watched some of the national aerobics championship. He closed all the cabinets in his house and, using his new drill, tightened all the hinges. He walked to the stationery shop to see if he could buy Adam anything. They didn't have much. He got a card congratulating him on his Bat Mitzvah, thinking that it was funny, knowing that Adam, who had to be told when to laugh, wouldn't get the joke.

Outside, it was summer. He bought a glass-blue Sno-Kone, wrapped in the same weak waxy paper they've been using for a hundred years, from a tiny man with a cart. He held it gingerly between his fingers. It was glorious, really too perfect to change. He didn't want to eat that ice—it was so right, that blue dome, like a tiny lost moon he could hold in his hand.

It began to melt, so he ate it in gulps.

He returned home, thinking maybe he should wait another day, or even two. The sooner he got there, really, the sooner Adam would feel well enough to leave the hospital, and the sooner he'd try it again. The longer Adam was in the hospital, probably restrained in some effective way, the better. He was content, Fish was sure. Adam was always content in a hospital.

At two-thirty, Fish called the rental place and they said they were on their way and could he give them his address again. He did, and waited.

At three o'clock, he called the place again and it was a new guy on the phone. New guy said he had no record of Fish's reservation. "You know," Fish said, "that's messed up. I've been waiting forever and I have to get down to goddamned Bakersfield." New guy sighed and said he'd look again. Then he got back on the phone and said that he was sorry, that he'd found the reservation posted on the bulletin board.

"*Someone*," he said, "put it up on the board without telling anyone else." He was directing this to some nameless offscreen coworker.

"Sure," Fish said, "but isn't that what the goddamned board is for, so you don't have to tell everyone about it?" Fish wanted a look at that office. "Jesus," he added. "That's really fucked."

"Well, I am sorry," new guy said.

"I have a friend in the hospital, motherfucker." Fish was surprised; he hadn't contemplated that sentence. He realized that this was one of those moments when one's impatience— or was the word *rage*?—was being misdirected. All the same, he thought he'd very much like to beat the new guy till he whispered.

New guy told Fish someone would come get him soon, and then hung up. Fish went into the tiny yellow yard in front of his house and took the croquet wickets out of the grass. They'd been sitting there for three months, since Mary's kids had been over. They couldn't play to save their lives, those kids. They didn't care about the rules, either. They just hit the balls like monkeys, squawking and swinging and running into the street.

Now it's seven o'clock, with two hours to go. This drive mocks our conceptions of time. This drive could kill anyone.

Adam's mouth curves too much. He's never been able to smile without smirking, or listen without sneering. It isn't his fault, really. He just has too many muscles there, in that area around his mouth. Most people are born handicapped.

He moved away, to Baltimore, just before high school, so Fish didn't see him much, but one summer, right after Adam's parents separated and he and Fish were too old for camp, Adam stayed with Fish's family in Galena. At first he slept in the basement, next to the dartboard and under the tiny window half-full of soil. When he complained about the ticking and groaning of the water heater, he was moved to Fish's bedroom. It was a small room with a single window, over Fish's bed, painted shut, the lower corners covered in stickers with holograms and google eyes.

That summer, when Adam played football with Fish's friends every Sunday at the muddy round park at the end of the frontage road, he tackled too hard and argued too much. Fish apologized for him. Everyone figured he was just intense, had something to prove, like the kids who'd tried out for the team but missed the last cut. Adam, though, was different, less in control, less focused on the outcome of the game.

He broke a guy's leg once. The weekend was warm; there were about twenty playing. One guy had borrowed cones from his construction job, and they figured they could have a proper game, with a kickoff even. So they split into sides and booted the ball. They started running like madmen at each other, and a boy named Catanese, older but spindly, everywhere elbows and knees, caught the kickoff, the ball delivering a thump to his concave chest.

He was running for the sideline, when Adam burst through the pack unblocked and just flew, for a frozen second almost perfectly horizontal, and finally spearing him, his shoulders plowing into Catanese's legs. There was a crack like a broken bat, and everyone cheered because Catanese was barely out of the end zone and his team would be screwed for field position. But then Catanese went red, blood swimming in his face, and he was holding his leg, one hand on either side, gently, like it was too hot to touch. He recoiled from it, screaming, out of his mind, feral.

The leg, the tibia, was snapped in two. It was a battlefield kind of gore, the bone poking through his corduroys like a stick through a garbage bag.

"You see that, what I did?" Adam said. Fish had found him up the hill, by the new playground, hiding in a chute. He thought Adam was going to brag about hitting Catanese so hard, but instead he said, "Why the hell would I break some kid's leg? What the hell is wrong with me?"

Fish told him that it was an accident, it wasn't his fault, it was football, a violent game, so what. Now Adam was pulling on the skin under his chin, grabbing it and pinching it. "I shouldn't play tackle," he said, pulling harder on his chin. "The craziest thing is that I've thought about something like this happening, you know?" Here he adopted a meaningful whisper. "I *knew* this would come to pass. When I get hold of someone I just get too... I feel like I want to tear them in half, know what I'm saying? Like I want to run through and get a bunch of people near me and then explode."

Fish nodded. Adam seemed to be horrified and proud and enthralled all at once. He had an aura that wasn't right, the wild glow of a scientist who'd discovered a formula that could kill millions.

The ambulance was loading Catanese now, and had pulled right up onto the field, which everyone thought was great; that had never happened before. Fish walked with Adam across the grass, now black and wet, without saying much. The light was almost gone, so they headed home, afraid of the night that

would soon bring Monday. Into the house, through the mud-
room, past Fish's parents playing Pong and up the stairs, Fish
quiet, now running his fingers over each baluster, while Adam
talked, sighed, touching nothing.

Fish finds a parking space under a wide wall of the hospital,
pink-bricked and bisected by the kind of steel ladder you see
on water towers—a fire escape, maybe. The grounds are lav-
ish, or seem so in the dark—cobblestone paths winding
around willows and palmettos, sprinklers hissing. As Fish is
walking in, a man in institutional blue holds the door for him.

"I assume you're a visitant?" he says.

"I don't know," Fish says.

"Of course you are. You have that radiant look."

The man giggles and Fish says thank you, unsure whether
or not to encourage him. He says thank you, tells the man, an
aide of some kind, where he's headed, and the aide, in his
scrubs and with plastic bags around his shoes, walks Fish all
the way to the Nursing/Trauma Unit. "I'd just confuse you
otherwise," he says. Fish isn't sure if that's an insult or what.

Adam is in Room 318, on the far side of the building. Fish
hopes he doesn't have a roommate, because the roommates in
hospitals are always deformed and either too sick or not sick
enough to be there in the first place. They listen to conversations and make judgments. But when he gets to the room
there's no roommate, just a twig of a woman, owlish and sal-
low, sitting on a chair near Adam, eating a brownie.

Fish waves hello to the brownie woman and walks around
to Adam. He lies flat, with a neck brace on, staring at the ceiling. Fish puts his face in Adam's line of vision.

"Hey," Adam says, surprised.

Fish grunts.

Adam doesn't look forty. He looks twelve. He's wearing a baseball cap, and his face isn't wrinkly or strung out or gaunt. With his freckles and the cap, he has the aura of a kid who's just had his tonsils out.

"What's the hat?" Fish asks. It bears a minor-league team's logo, a beaver holding a bat he's apparently been chewing on.

"What are you doing here?" Adam asks. His eyes open a little more, catching the glare of a car's headlights in the parking lot.

"Who gave it to you?" Fish says.

"One of the nurses. Ronnie."

"Do you get to keep it, or is it just for here?"

"I don't know. I think I can keep it. Did you drive down?"

"Yeah."

"Wow. Thanks, man."

"That's a bitch of a drive," Fish says.

"I *know*," he says with what Fish considers an appropriate amount of awe and gratitude. "Sorry. Thanks."

On his mobile table are remnants of dinner or lunch or both—uneaten tapioca and two tangelos, and beside them a little tilting pagoda of Tupperware. The lady with the brownie has finished with the brownie and is now cleaning her nails with a thumbtack. Fish nods to Adam and jerks his head toward her. She has a hospital I.D. tag clipped to her blouse.

"She sits here with me," he says. "They've got someone in here all the time so I don't do anything." It's clear that Adam is happy they think he's such a serious customer, such a dangerous man. Fish looks over at the brownie woman to see if she's listening, but she isn't; she's watching a movie on Adam's TV—Fred Thompson is playing the president, and is wearing that dissatisfied look he uses. Fish stares out the window. In the parking lot, the cars are colored copper by the light from above, the lamps bent over them like tall thin saints over babies. He sees his rental and misses being inside it.

Adam is holding a little tube with a button on it.

"Is that for morphine?" Fish asks.

"Yeah," Adam says.

"So you try to jump off a building, and they give you morphine—an unlimited amount?"

"No. I can only get a certain amount each hour. They've got it figured out."

Fish knows it's just a matter of time before Adam starts telling him why he jumped off the motel roof, but he doesn't want to hear it. *Oh, if only it were interesting!* he thinks. But it never is. "I wanted to hurt myself," he will say, "I don't know why." Nothing of any interest will get said by either of them. Adam will say, "I feel so dark sometimes" or "It's like I see things sometimes... through a dark water." Adam wants Fish to understand, but Fish isn't interested, and, besides, he'll call Adam on where he stole that dark-water part—*The Executioner's Song,* Adam's favorite book—and remind him of a hundred ways the two of them, Fish and Adam, are equal in this *darkness.* They've seen the same things, they have the same urges. Adam will concede this, and will begin apologizing for everything, and for too long. He'll be too contrite, too docile, and Fish will want to step on him.

But at some point they'll start making plans for when Adam is discharged. This is the only part that ever interests Fish: the steps from here on out. Fish will get inspired, laying out what will happen in the first few days, the weeks after, every move for years. First, a different apartment in a new city, away from the therapist-criminals in Bakersfield who keep prescribing drugs, every conceivable drug, for Adam. Then a

menial job while doing some kind of night school, and finally
a woman, older, hardened, wise, but warm—who will tie him
to a pole in the basement when he needs it. Or what he really
needs is a man. He needs a burly man, a hairy gay man who
goes to *bear* bars. He'd give Adam love and respect but also be
paternal, stern, watchful enough to save Adam from himself.

"So how's Mary?" Adam asks.

"She's good," Fish says.

"Where's she living now?"

"I can't tell you."

"She's my cousin. You can't tell me where she lives?"

"No."

"Why?"

"Because she's got little kids, Adam, and you're a guy who
shoots himself and jumps off roofs. Fuck you."

For a second Adam looks hurt, or pretends to look hurt,
then he closes his eyes. Fish fears that he's just made Adam feel
more unique and menacing—precisely what Adam wants.

His chin is brown and tied together with black straight
string, spiked along the suture, as if spiders had been sewn
into his face.

"Ow. Don't," Adam says.

Fish is touching the stitches.

"Why not?"

"Stop it, prick."

"How many?" It's like a cactus or something. The stitches
are amazing.

"Twelve. Get the fuck away."

Fish gives him a look.

"Sorry," Adam says. But he has no rights here. After five
hours of driving, Fish is allowed to touch what he wants. Fish
remembers the card and drops it on Adam's chest. Adam tries

to look down at it.

"You have to hold it up. I can't see."

Fish opens it and shows him the front. It's an elephant surrounded by Hebrew letters, with "Happy Bat Mitzvah" written below.

"A Jewish elephant," Adam says.

"I guess so," Fish says.

Fish used to like hospitals. Waiting rooms in particular. When his last girlfriend, Annie, had her appendix out, he was at the hospital for thirty hours and had a pretty good time. He met people, learned things—there was some strange collegial vibe that night. Three of them played cards and Fish won a hundred and twenty-two dollars on a straight flush from a guy whose brother was getting a finger reattached. He'd been drilling a hole through his son's wall, thought the kid was selling crystal meth and wanted to catch him. That had been a good night.

But with Adam he doesn't want to stay. Fish looks at the clock. It says 8:40. He'll leave at nine, he decides. Then he'll call Annie to see if he can stay with her for the night. Annie follows local politics and has ridiculous lips, full like balloon animals, a voice lower than his. The last time Fish saw her she scratched his head so masterfully, in circles so convincing, that he thought he was rising, ascending. They talk often enough, and she lives in L.A., and he figures he'll drive over after, not for sex or even romance, just for a place to rest where there's breathing other than his own, where he won't have to leave the TV on all night. If she's not around he'll drive back to San Jose tonight. He could do it. Through the night is easier.

"Does your mom know?" Fish asks. He knows that Adam's mom doesn't know, because Adam told Chuck that if she found out he'd do it for real next time.

"No. I don't think so," Adam says.

Adam's father died a few years ago, a botched bypass, and now his mother lives in Australia. She went there with a man she'd met in a community-theater production of *Fiorello!* He played the lead, though he was six feet four and blond.

A nurse comes in. She's Filipina, young. Her nametag says "Hope." Fish feels an urge to say something about her name, in light of her working in a hospital and all, but then figures she hears that often enough.

"That's a good name for a nurse," he says. What the hell.

She takes Adam's blood pressure. Fish watches, loving how quickly the armband fills with air, how tight it gets. That device always looks like something illegal.

"How's your pain?" she asks Adam.

"Good," Adam says.

The nurse takes the Bat Mitzvah card off Adam's stomach and puts it on the side table, next to a jar of denim-colored tools, like lollipops but with foam starfish tops. Cleaning devices, maybe, for swabbing mouths or other wet orifices. Fish thinks briefly about taking one of the lollipops and stuffing it up Adam's fat fucking nose. He almost laughs at the thought of it.

Fish leaves while Adam is drifting in and out, his face blank, almost beatific. During a brief moment when his eyes pull open, Fish tells him he'll check in again tomorrow.

The night is sharp, all the lights crisp, and Fish drives to the motel where Chuck said Adam had been staying. He's supposed to pick up Adam's things—four bags' worth. Adam had been living there for a month, after he was asked to leave his halfway house for skinning a chicken in his room. That's what

Chuck said, at least. If Adam did indeed skin a chicken, he did it only to say he'd done it. "Ask for Mr. Ali," Chuck said. Chuck handled logistics. He was Adam's attorney, benefactor, medical historian. Fish was someone who could drive down and pick up bags.

When he gets to the motel, a women's volleyball team is checking in. He waits for twenty minutes while they decide who will sleep in whose rooms, and which duffels will stay in the minibus. Fish reads every brochure the lobby offers, and makes a tentative plan to see the Museum of Irrigation.

When it's his turn Fish asks for Mr. Ali, but the woman at the counter, heavy-lidded and wearing a maize-colored sari, says he's gone. "I am Mrs. Ali. Yes please?" Fish shows her the letter that Chuck faxed, asking for Adam's stuff. Chuck insisted on ending the letter with "I trust that this matter will not present a problem." Every legal letter Chuck writes ends this way. He loses half of his cases.

Fish can see the bags just behind her, in a narrow hallway with a cement floor. Two clear plastic bags sit there, alert, and two tennis bags, one covered in mud. Mrs. Ali reads the note, then looks up at Fish. It's then that he almost cries. Water seems to fill his forehead; his eyes are just portals that show he's drowning. What is she looking at? How much does she know? She must know. The ambulance picked Adam up here, and she or her husband surely packed and stored his belongings. She knew Adam as a flailer, as a leaper, and now knows Fish as someone lesser, someone who picks up the bags of people like Adam. Fish is now among the people who live in motels and jump off motel roofs. There's a highway just above the motel, and on it people are passing this place at eighty miles an hour, wondering what happens in the filthy world below.

"I have to call Mr. Ali," she says, and does so, using a

receiver larger than her face. She gets off the phone with Mr. Ali and lets Fish into the hallway behind the desk.

"Thanks," he says on the way out.

"All right," she says, opening the door for him. "Good!" she adds, and after he's gone throws the bolt, right to left.

Fish loads the bags into his trunk, and then remembers what he wanted to investigate. He has forgotten to look until now, and is suddenly thrilled. He walks over to the courtyard area to see where Adam jumped. But he can't find a part of the motel complex that has four stories. There is just the one two-story building, in an L shape around the pool, and its roof is only about eighteen feet high. *Dumbshit!* Fish has figured it out. Of course! Forty feet isn't Adam's way, after all, but eighteen feet is. He jumped from this. *Dumbshit! Coward! Pissfuck!* Who jumps eighteen feet? Who does this? This is so wrong. There are too many things wrong everywhere for this kind of thing, this jumping from eighteen-foot roofs. Adam must have known that eighteen feet wasn't far enough to kill himself, just far enough to break bones. And the only thing sadder than an eighteen-foot motel roof is the guy staring at it.

He goes back to the car and opens the trunk. He reaches inside one of the plastic bags, looking for something solid. Most of its contents are soft, clothes, and here and there moist, but he soon finds a trophy, a small one with a tennis player on top and someone else's name engraved on it. Elsewhere between the folds of shirts and socks there is some deodorant, a handful of tapes, which Fish pulls out for the drive home, and a bottle of cologne called Together, which makes him laugh. Adam is the only guy Fish knows who wears cologne. The only other items of note are five belts, wound as one like a rat-tlesnake, and a ten-pound container of baby powder.

And now a woman is walking across the lot toward Fish.

Every part of her is moving—her ankles, unsteady in heels; her
arms swinging; her head, which jitters with each step, as if it,
too, played a part in her propulsion. Her features are mis-
matched—small chin, wide nose, the icy, almost clear eyes of
a wolf. She's wearing jeans and a denim jacket, with pointy
blue velveteen boots and the streamlined, utilitarian body of a
tomboy teenager.

"Hi," she says.

"Hi," Fish says.

"What're you doing?" she asks. "Coming or going?"

She reminds him of the South somehow. He thinks of
Kentucky and doesn't know why. Is she nineteen or thirty?
Fish can't tell.

"I'm packing this stuff up," he says.

"Then?"

"Then I'm driving down to see a friend." It's after ten and
he hasn't called Annie yet. If he calls too late she won't let him
come over.

"Can you give me a ride?" the woman says. "I'm trying to
get to San Diego."

"Oh. Yeah. See, I'm not going that far."

Behind them, a truck parks and sighs.

"I can get out wherever you stop."

He looks at her to see if she has a gun or a crowbar. He
wants to help, but more than this, he wants to leave. Not long
ago, at a gas station in Daly City, a tall man in a straw hat told
Fish that he didn't have any cash, and could Fish spot him
twenty dollars—he'd give Fish a personal check in exchange.
Fish figured he'd be less than human if he said no, so he said
yes. The man had a car, after all, and was wearing a sports coat,
so this was just a small transaction between solvent citizens.
The guy put his home phone number on the check and every-

thing. But the check bounced.

Fish had only wanted to help the man. He spent that first day thinking he had helped him, believing in the community of souls, in Daly City or anywhere. And then that man took it away. He reached inside Fish and took that from him.

Fish gets in the car and unlocks the passenger side. He moves a Jack in the Box bag and a milk carton and now the woman is sitting in the passenger seat, a few inches from him. She picks up the map from the floor, folds it quickly, expertly, and puts it in the side compartment.

"Thanks for this. You're sweet," she says, giving him her hand in a royal way. "What's your name?"

"Eddie," he says. Her hand is cold. He doesn't know if he should kiss it or shake it. He doesn't do either, just holds it for a few seconds and lets it drop.

"That's weird," she says. "My brother's name is Eddie. Was."

Now Fish considers giving her his real name. Instead, he says, "He changed his name?"

"No, he died."

"Oh. I'm sorry."

"No worries," she says.

Fish pulls out of the parking lot and onto the frontage road. No worries. He wants to tell her how much he hates that expression, but doesn't. "Don't worry" makes sense, is a pat on the arm, a reassurance from one person to another, but "No worries" implies there aren't any worries anywhere in the world, and that's just not true.

They get on the highway. Fish asks her name. Her name is Wendy.

"Where're you going?" she asks.

"Redondo Beach, I think." That's where Annie lives. Near the beach, with a futon, in a cave of an apartment next to the garage of a family of five. Her place is full of small glass figurines of mythical animals, ears pinched while the glass was molten— hippogriffs, hydras, satyrs, a tiny sphinx the color of cantaloupe.

"My ex lives in Redondo," Wendy says. "He's married now. She had four kids. Two of them Downies."

"Huh," Fish says. She is staring at him. He wonders how he looks in profile.

"So what were you doing at the motel?"

"Nothing. Getting stuff."

"What stuff?"

"Just some stuff. Friend's stuff." Somehow that sounds shady. But he lets it go. She seems impressed.

Wendy pushes the radio scan button a few times, and finds the "Oooh-oooh, Jackie Blue" song.

"I love this song," she says, and slaps her lap loudly. She leaves her hands there, grabbing her thighs as if to keep them in place.

"So do you party?" she asks.

"What?"

"Do. You. Party."

"In general? I don't—"

"You know. Party."

He's lost. He gives her a pleading look.

"You and me, party, handsome. We should go party some- where. We could stop and get a drink and stuff. Or a room. Get some weed. Whatever."

Fish finally knows. Shit. Normal women don't call men "handsome"—only waitresses and prostitutes do that. It's a shame, though. "Handsome" is such a beautiful word.

Fish gives her offer some thought. Her thighs have his head lunging. But it would cost too much, right, spending time with a woman like this? He doesn't know. *How did I get to my age without knowing how much things like this cost?* But he can't. He never takes off his shirt with people he doesn't know. She'd see the hair on his shoulders and his hernia scar, much more sinister than it needed to be and she'd think he was a bad package, that the hair and the crooked smiling scar were proof he needed to pay for the kind of company she could offer.

"Nah, I gotta get down to Redondo," he says, as if deciding whether or not to see an afternoon movie. "My friend's waiting for me. And his wife and my mom and everyone. Cousins." His mouth is adding family members quicker than his head can count. "They're probably all waiting up."

"We can be quick, if you want," she says.

Another orange-and-black bird appears, shooting across the road low and fast. Fish wants to ask Wendy if she knows what they're called—thrushes? finches? Not that it would make any difference, knowing their name. A name is a diagnosis, and neither makes a bit of difference. He glances over at her; her shoulders are squared to him now, her chin lowered. "I'm not expensive," she says.

Fish pulls off the highway and under a gas-station canopy; it's bright like daylight and he thinks of Reno. Wendy has asked to use the bathroom, and here her skin looks blue, translucent, as if lit from within, and the humidity has lifted. Instead of using the bathroom, though, she heads straight to the pay phone, and while she's on the phone she waves Fish away like he's her father dropping her off at a concert. He leaves.

By the time he gets to a phone to call Annie, it's too late.

He wakes her up, or she pretends to have been asleep. Her first syllable is full of scorn, and he wonders if Wendy is still at the gas station where he left her, a few miles back. "You have to start thinking of other people, honey," Annie says, now without anger, without anything, and hangs up.

He is back at the hospital twenty minutes later. It's well after midnight, and he has no hope of getting up to Adam's room through the doors. He parks his car in the same spot and calculates which window is his. He knows that Adam is on the third floor, and the two possible windows are on either side of the steel ladder. So he runs under the willows and through the palmettos and starts up.

It's the left window. He can see Adam in the light of the TV. His twelve-year-old's face is facing Fish now, eyes closed. The brownie woman has gone.

As Fish is about to tap on the glass, Adam opens his eyes. When he sees Fish, he's disbelieving. He closes one eye, as if looking through a telescope, to be sure. Fish waves, and Adam, with his fingers only, waves back.

Fish hasn't thought any further than this. If he had a specific message for Adam, he could mime it through the glass, but he doesn't have that kind of message.

Adam mouths the word "How?" and points to Fish. Fish is about to mime climbing a ladder but realizes he can't do this without taking both hands off the rungs. He tries it with one hand, but it looks more like he's shopping, like he's doing the shopping-cart dance. Adam doesn't get it.

Fish shakes his head, wiping the board clean. He decides he'll pry the window open and tumble in and talk. But the window frame is flush to the building. It will not give.

Fish knocks his head on the glass, twice. Adam smiles. Fish does it a few more times, just to entertain him. Adam pretends to be laughing a lot. It isn't as great as either of them makes it out to be, but there isn't anything else to do. Soon Adam yawns. Fish yawns. Adam's eyes are flickering, so Fish gestures that he'll see him tomorrow, rolling his hand like he's creating a wave, the wave meaning tomorrow, rolling and rolling.

Fish drives to Redondo and checks into a Red Roof by the highway. He figures he'll call Annie in the morning and then see Adam again on his way back north, and do something with all the bags after he's gone through them and dumped the pills and anything else he doesn't want Adam to have. He resolves to get him a real suitcase or two, something with a hard shell, sturdy. He can do that tomorrow.

Tomorrow!

Tomorrow he can put Adam's stuff in the sturdy suitcases and take them to him, put them in the hospital room, lined up by the door so they're there when he's ready to leave. Adam can be a promising young man with neat sturdy suitcases. Fish will repack everything, put it all in two rows, pants on one side and shirts on the other, with the second suitcase holding the other things—socks and underwear and toiletries and belts, baby powder. Tomorrow he can do these things better than he did today. Tomorrow! Tomorrow!

Fish's Red Roof room is dark and he knows he's being stupid. The walls smell like people, and he doesn't deserve this, to be tricked like this again. He had made so many promises to himself that he would never waste himself, never again hand a pure intention, so much like a newborn, to someone so careless. He is done being fooled. Why would that Daly City man jack him on a bad check? It was such violence. He will not be the sucker. He doesn't want to be a part of the world under the highway. No. Today was tomorrow and tomorrow was always the same. No, he'll skip Annie and Adam and just get a shotgun now and go to that farm on I-5 and shoot a bunch of stupid cows. Ha ha! They wouldn't make it, anyway—so many animals are built to die. Maybe cut off their heads and hollow them out and wear one as a mask. Yes! Just for fun. Just to do it. The humidity inside one of those big heavy heads—he'd love to see what it's like in there for a second. His clean hair would be covered in blood, his face wet, filthy from the stuff he didn't scoop out before he put the fucking thing on.

SHE WAITS, SEETHING, BLOOMING

SHE IS A SINGLE MOTHER and has no interest in any men but her son, who is fifteen and has not called. It is 2:33 am and he hasn't phoned since 5:40 that evening, when he said he'd be eating dinner out. And now she is watching *Elimidate*, drinking red wine spiked with gin, and is picturing hitting her only son with a golf club. She is picturing slapping him flat and hard across his face and is thinking that the sound it would make would almost make up for her worry, her inability to sleep, the many hundreds of dire thoughts that have torched her mind these past hours. Where is he? She doesn't even know where he would go, or with whom. He's a loner, he's an eccentric. He is, she thinks, the sort of teenager who gets involved with deviants on the Internet. And yet somehow she knows that he is safe, that he is fine but has for whatever reason been unable to call, or has not even given it much thought. He is testing his boundaries, perhaps, and she will remind him of the consequences of such thoughtlessness. And when she thinks of what she will say to him and how loudly she will say it, she feels a strange kind of pleasure. The pleasure is like that enjoyed by the passionate scratching of a body overwhelmed with irritation. Giving oneself up to that scratching, everywhere and furious—which she did only a month earlier when she'd contracted poison oak—that was the most profound pleasure she had ever known. And now, waiting for her son and knowing how righteous will be her indignation, how richly justified will be anything she yells into his irresponsible face, she finds herself awaiting his arrival in the way the ravenous might await a meal. She is nodding her head. She is tapping a pen against her dry lips. She tries to order her thoughts, to decide where to start with him. How general should her criticisms be? Should they be specific only to this night, or should this be the door through which they pass in order to talk about all of his failings? The possibilities! She will have license to go anywhere, to say anything. She pours more gin into her tumbler of merlot, and when she looks up, at 2:47, his headlights are drawing chalk across the front window. This will be divine, she thinks. This will be superb. It will be florid, glorious; she will scratch and scratch and bloom. She runs to the door. She can't wait for it to begin.

QUIET

THE LAST TIME I told this story, I ended it with a conversation I had with the nickly shimmer of the moon on a black lake on the Isle of Skye. It went like this:

"You are a lucky one, Tom, to have Erin and others like Erin." The voice of the nickly reflection of the moon was not as deep as you might expect. It was a singer's voice, though, a tenor, one that loved itself without reservation.

"Thank you," I said. "I feel blessed."

"I often think of coming down to live among you, to make a big mess of it all," he said. "It always looks so messy, and I think I might like that."

"It is messy, I guess."

"It looks *awfully* messy. It looks almost impossible to survive, to tell you the truth. The pain of it all."

"It's not all that painful," I said.

"But Tom," it said, "the swinging of your pendulums! Everyone's pendulums swinging, to and fro, and always you're getting hit by someone else's swinging pendulum. You're minding your business, but someone else's pendulum is swinging around, and pow! you get it in the head."

"That happens, yes."

"I saw you and Erin by the shed."

"Oh."

"I was there."

"That makes sense. I saw you, too."

"I watch you often, Tom. I have time on my hands. Time is different to me than it is to you."

I was still thinking about what the nickly shimmer had seen. He, however, was warming to the sound of his thoughts.

"I feel time like you dream. Your dreams are jumbled. You can't remember the order of your dreams, and when you recall them, the memories bend. Faces change. It's all in puddles and ripples. That's what time is for me."

Three days earlier, at the airport, I was stunned that Erin had actually shown up. That she'd really come. That she had a car. "And you can drive on the other side? Do they do that up here, too?" "They do. I do." She looked good. Pale. She had a long nose, bent a bit, seeming almost broken, working in perfect concert with her exquisitely thick chocolate hair, hair like it had been brushed a thousand times by magic elves.

I have always been the good friend. I have been harmless, listening, waiting.

"You look so much better," she said to me.

"Thanks," I said, not knowing what she meant.

I had flown out for a long weekend, and she and I planned to drive to the Isle of Skye. We hugged and I groaned into her sweater, pulled back and looked at her more. Her eyes still the blue of oceans on maps. She still had dark freckles, almost spots, really, round and discrete, sprayed over and around her nose and cheeks. I depended on those, and loved her old coffee-colored jeans, flared a little, faded over her bold, assertive backside—she'd been in a college production of a play about Robert Crumb's women. Such a triumph she was—and so how had I, with my shapeless torso and oily neck, been allowed to get so close? I stood and bounced on my toes and tried not to sweat or scream or lift her and carry her around on my shoulder.

Edinburgh was raining and dark at noon. I was baffled that Erin—Erin Mahatma Fullerton—was so confident here, when she'd left me and D.C. only a year before. That she could drive on the wrong side of the road with such confidence.

"You're incredible," I said, about her driving. "How do you not mess it up? How are we not dead?"

"I guess I'm just used to being good at everything."

She was good at everything. I couldn't remember anything she couldn't do well. I wasn't jealous about this. I was not threatened. I should be able to just make a statement like that without being judged.

She drove with her hand on the wheel, not really gripping it, her wrist resting on top. I reached over and squeezed her knee.

"This is so weird," she said, then laughed by throwing her head all the way forward. It was the first time I'd seen her do that.

"I know," I said. "But good, right?"

"Yeah, good. It's good." She laughed again the same way. Each time she did this she almost hit her face on the steering wheel. It was a new and fake habit—at what age do we stop acquiring affectations like that? I hoped she wouldn't do it again, because if she did I would have to ask her to stop.

We'd met at a protest, or on the way to one, a confused and desperate event. It was supposed to be an anti-IMF/World Bank march, but had been fashioned into an action against the potential bombing of Afghanistan. This was in September.

Blocks away I first caught sight of her pants, violet-blue, and followed her quickly and asked if she were heading to Freedom Plaza. She said yes. She was friendly enough, accepting my companionship for the walk there. She said she was curious only, didn't want to get too close to the demonstration, being an employee of the Treasury and all.

I laughed. Was she serious? She was. What was her area of work? She worked as a liaison between Treasury and the IMF. I laughed again. I'd never met anyone from Treasury.

"Hold on," she said. She stood, her knuckle on her lips.

I stared at the knuckle on her lips. Something happened then that should not have been possible: a tiny bird alighted on her shoulder. Erin was unsurprised.

"Well zippety-do-da!" she said to the bird. "Isn't that strange?" she said to me.

The bird departed and Erin led me through a short cut. Under a marble archway and through an outdoor mall we walked. I dipped my fingers into a small fountain, the water too warm. We passed a Cartier shop on the right as the sounds of the protest became louder, somewhere above our heads. Before us were a set of polished steps and to our left the park. I followed her.

There was something experimental about her, I thought, physically. She didn't seem to have a left arm. We walked down the steps, and I was on her right side, so I wasn't in a position to know more.

I leaned forward and confirmed that there was no left arm swinging, no left hand at her side. I was growing more certain that she had only one arm. A large black minivan stopped in front of us, and in the window I saw her reflection clearly. Four cops or agents in riot gear stepped out, hulking, sullen, and Erin was missing an arm. The effect wasn't something ruined or feeble, though, was somehow harmonious—not a handicap but just a viable variation. Instead of allowing her one sleeve to dangle, she'd sewn it at the shoulder. Or the manufacturer had. It was seamless. She saw me looking. She turned and walked.

Did people look at Erin strangely? It depended on their angle, first of all. Those who could grasp and be certain that she was missing a limb might cock their heads or pause briefly. Not out of revulsion. It was more like simple surprise, as when you see identical twins, adults, dressed alike, or a cat on a leash. I wanted to be closer to her because she seemed like the future to me, like a new sort of person, a new species. When I was thirteen I'd had a friend, half French and half Vietnamese, who had given me the same feeling of satisfaction—bridging the gap between my world and the one I thought was new.

On the peripheries of the protest was a smattering of TV cameras, trolling. We watched while demonstrators wandered into and out of the plaza. It wasn't clear if the protest was beginning or ending or in full swing. The energy was mild. The ratio of protesters to those documenting them was roughly one to one.

"You don't seem very happy," she said to me.

This made me happy. I smiled. I felt like a bird that had
landed on her shoulder. She was unspoiled land on which I
could settle. I could bring everything I had.

I asked her if she worried about losing her job, if she was
caught on film. I put my knuckle to my lips.

"Not really," she said. "There are lots of jobs. There are so
many things to do. Too damned many, really. It might be time
to move anyway. This town is choking me."

She laughed with her eyes closed. I laughed and watched
her. I knew then that I would get her a job where I worked,
that she and I would become closer, that I would know the
things I wanted to know about her.

We sat on the curb.

Near us a bearded man's sign said "Friend of the Earth."

Erin pointed to him. "He's a friend of the Earth," she said.

A couple walked by, young and holding hands, wearing
black handkerchiefs over their faces. Erin's face darkened.
"I have to get out of this country for a while," she said.

That was more than two years ago. Now, in our small plastic-
smelling car we skittered around Edinburgh's glowering black
fortress. Up the hill and through the castle's parking lot running and squealing in the rain and once within the thick stone
walls we took a tour elucidating the history of the country's
crown jewels. We made very, very funny jokes about these
crown jewels, and the role of the peasant women in protecting
and hiding them. We watched footage of Scottish soldiers
from WWII, maybe it was WWI, though most of the film
involved the soldiers standing around smoking pipes. The old
speedy film made them seem nervous, their movements bird-
like. There was a long stretch of the soldiers in kilts, dancing

two by two, arms hooked, on an outdoor stage, presumably to entertain their colleagues. Spinning, twirling, sometimes with one hand above their heads, sometimes one over their bellies—it's hard to explain.

"They don't teach soldiers to dance like they used to," Erin said.

Every man in the film was dead by now. When I was very young I couldn't watch anything black and white on TV because I knew the people moving were now dust. I hugged Erin from behind, and she stared at my hands linked, loosely, over around her waist.

I knew that she had not been content since moving to London. Her worries, though, came from home. She was getting news from her family and felt helpless. Her favorite cousin, a marine, was in Kabul. Her parents were still married but were seeing other people; her mother was dating a retired man who held the Stop sign at a school crosswalk. He sat on a lawn chair when between trips across the road.

"I always assumed he wasn't all there," Erin said, about the man, whose name was Jedediah. "Not retarded, you know..." She made a face that looked like a zombie's. She scratched her temples and crossed her eyes. Now the man was sleeping in her mother's bed.

I'd never been interested in someone like Erin before. She had an MBA, which I didn't understand—MBAs generally or the fact that she'd wanted one. She knew menus and cheeses and Caribbean islands named after saints. But she was very strong and even reckless. She had quit her job in D.C. and now she was here.

She wanted to start an ex-pat community in London, or Scotland or Ireland. Or Norway. She hadn't made up her mind, and was auditioning possible locations—somewhere, she said, "where all the churches aren't covered in scaffolding." Skye was among the candidates. She'd just been to Montenegro and was disappointed. "I expected more mustaches," she said. "Mustaches and fedoras."

I had the feeling that she'd overromanticized the idea of living elsewhere, but I didn't tell her this. We stepped through the castle museum, so many old things behind new glass. She complained that she was losing friends to substances and babies, that she was fighting, over the phone, with everyone she knew in the U.S. She was convinced she was right each time, but still, she wanted to know if she seemed insane. I told her she was perfect.

"I'm always on your side," I said.

"Fine. You stay close, and together we'll systematically remove all the crazies from my life."

The car didn't have a CD player but Erin had an adapter that connected her portable disc player to the tape deck. While she drove us down the hill and into the town, I hooked everything up, only to find that the wires wouldn't stay connected without some kind of adhesive.

"Hold on," she said.

She stopped the car at a small market on the back end of the castle and ran in. It was the first time we'd been apart since the airport, and it was too soon. I put my hand on the leather where she'd been sitting. I wanted it to be warmer.

She jogged back to the car grinning like she'd stolen something The door opened, rain and wind scrambled in loudly, and she came inside. The door closed behind her with a clump.

"Guess what I just bought?" she asked.

I guessed: "Tape."

"Riiiiight…" She was twirling her index finger in the air, pulling more words from my mouth, like winding a yo-yo. It drove me half-mad with desire.

"Special tape?" I ventured, wanting to take her face and squeeze it and lick it.

"Not just tape. Scotch tape."

"Right."

"Get it, *Scotch* tape?"

"Oh."

The rain pattered.

She pulled it out of the white paper bag with a flourish. I widened my eyes, trying to seem impressed.

The tape was yellowed, an amber sort of color. It looked like the tape we'd used in grade school, before they invented good tape.

"It looks old," I said.

"No, no, this is the best. They invented it, these people! Probably up there, in that castle. A bunch of monks, took them centuries." She was desperately trying to get some tape from the roll but it wasn't attached to any standard tape dispensing device. I wanted to help but knew she'd ask me if she felt she needed it. That was the rule.

In a few seconds she was done assembling, wrapping the tape around the adapter and the walkman. But the tape wasn't sticking. It fell off immediately. It was like paper. It was not tape. It had no adhesive qualities whatsoever.

I laughed and then stopped. She was angry. She peeled off another strip and tested its stickiness against her fingers.

"It's not even sticky," she said. "I can't believe it."

She started the car and pulled out.

"This is *Scotch tape*, right?" she said. "God *damn* it."

* * *

Up through the highlands at dusk. Throughout the electric-green hills were great white stones flung like teeth.

"I see this and I think glory," I said to Erin, loving the sound of the word *glory*, and hoping it would impress her in some way. I was driving now, and soon realized that driving on the wrong side wasn't very difficult.

"I'd love to live here," I said, trying to sound dreamy.

"You can't live here," she said. "There's nothing here. No work."

"I could telecommute."

Silence from Erin.

"If you were here," I started, then dropped the thought.

She gave me a fake smile. I soaked up every ounce of it.

When I met Erin I was working at a statistics-processing firm, a small shop founded by a one-time major league pitcher named Dean Denny. He was a side-armer, goofy and musta-chioed. After retiring at thirty-two, he'd run for office, lost, spent ten years as a lobbyist for everyone from Exxon to Greenpeace, then started the American Institute for Statistical Studies. The firm was located in a converted Victorian in Alexandria, catering to the nonprofits in D.C., some federal agencies, and those who wanted influence at either or both. The other two staff members were Michael and Derek, Michael being Dean's son and Derek being Michael's old friend and the former personal assistant to Alan Simpson, sen-ator of Wyoming.

Two months after meeting Erin I secured a job for her at the AISS. I was afraid she'd hate Michael and Derek, that they would drive her away. For their own amusement, they had recently removed one letter from the firm's name and had made business cards with A.S.S. on them. They were chucklers, they were assholes. They called me The Turtle.

Then Turtle-man.

Then Yertle.

Then Yentl. Then Lentil.

Finally they went back to Turtle.

They were funny and loyal. They laughed about Dockers but then wore pants shockingly close to Dockers. Sometimes they'd wear baseball caps to work, the bill carefully bent in an upside-down grin, the edges frayed. Their footwear was always perfect—old Nike hiker's low-tops in earth tones, or white bucks flawlessly faded and scuffed. They dressed the way certain Cape Coddish catalogs tried to dress their models, but these two were better at it, effortless about it, tucking one side of their shirts in just so, their clothes worn in but never threadbare—

It sounds as though I was paying attention to their wardrobe but I don't remember it that way. You know these men. They're fine people, they know right from wrong. I had a strong feeling that, in a pinch, they would do more for me than I would for them. It was more in their blood; they were not people who would think twice.

The American Institute for Statistical Studies was the only one of its kind on the East Coast and therefore we were the best at what we did. We were the people who took the statistics— how many people injured on the job each year, how many boys fondled by priests every decade, how many cats declawed in urban areas every week, anything—and, among other services, extrapolated those numbers into the frequency per day, per hour, minute, whatever seemed most grievous. We knew all the pertinent figures—525,600 minutes in a year, 31,536,000

seconds—and so could always figure out how to make whatever issue or trend seem as menacing as possible. Three million squirrels poisoned by processed food a year is one thing,
but if the public knows that one such squirrel dies every
twelve seconds, well then, the reasoning goes, you have a pop-
ulace motivated to act.

Given our physical proximity, the four of us knew an inor-
dinate amount about each other. We could hear, if we chose to
listen, every word spoken by any of the others, on the phone
or otherwise. We quickly became protective of one another
but especially of Erin, who we pretended needed our shield-
ing. She had been raised as an only child outside of
Asheville—she had the faintest accent—and now she felt, she
often said, as if she'd inherited three brothers. When she first
said that, after we'd been working together for a few months,
we three coveted it, being thought of as her brothers—it
prompted Derek, at least, to start lifting weights. But it made
anyone's romantic pursuit of Erin seem against nature or God.
We'd all had, before that point, intentions of varying severity.
My feelings for Erin were confused. I loved her.

She noticed things about me. When I sat across from her, at
any meal, she would find a time, after looking at me for a few
seconds, to make a declaration. "You have minnow-shaped eyes,"
she said. "You smell clean. Like a little boy," she said. It didn't
matter what she said, I was always grateful. "You have something below you," she said to me, eating a hoagie one day, pry-
ing open my every pore and reading my every memory. "Like a
bunch of teeth waiting to come through."

I wanted to love her heroically, selflessly—to honor her
and defend her, and punish people who looked at her stump in
a way that displeased her. But soon I realized that she had
more than enough suitors, and at least a few of them would be

better for her. They all seemed to be quiet, uncomplicated
men, who were usually older and who invariably looked older
than they were, and wore wool. But occasionally we glimpsed
an "old friend" or an acquaintance from this gym or that
band—she went to a lot of shows—and these men caused us
concern. These men were thinner, unshaven, wore boots.

She spread her attention between the three of us with
maddening equability. We usually all ate together, but occasionally, in a casual but calculated rotation, we ate with her
alone. For a time, Michael and Derek stepped into an area
where they were permitted to make ribald jokes about her
missing arm. I never followed, nor did Dean. Derek she
allowed to call her Lefty, but at some point Michael lost his
license to kid her about the arm, I don't know how. I rejoiced.

Michael, Derek, and I, each unsure of the others' intentions and of our own, agreed, drunkenly one night, never to
touch her, not even in a state like the one in which we cur-
rently found ourselves. Everyone had their intimacies, though.
Derek took her on motorcycle rides, Michael taught her how
to roast a pig. I was the one—either because she loved me more
or because I was the least virile—she told about her men.

She claimed never to want to talk much about them, but
she did, with little provocation. Hearing their names, or the
nicknames she gave them—Fingers, Señor con Queso, Mr.
Robinson—made me uneasy; it was clear that many of them
were still lurking nearby, and that she was not adept at or will-
ing to cut them loose. She lamented the fact that she seemed
to attract men who wanted to *extract* something from her. She
used this word, *extract*, often, when talking about these
unnamed men. I considered her flawless, though I wished she
were more careful, or better able to keep herself out of the path
of these bad men. The bad men, I told her, were not always

obvious at first, though I wasn't sure that was true.

"I can't worry about the intentions of everyone I know," she said.

"Wrong," I said. "You *have* to worry about their intentions. Within three minutes of meeting any man, his intentions toward you are decided, completely."

"I don't believe that," she said.

Stopped at an outcropping, a mist swirled around us as if it were going to leave a genie in its wake, and when it lifted, I hugged Erin, my front to her back. I buried my head in her neck. She accepted this, and turned to face me, and then held me with a quick intensity—and let go. She knew I was weak and stupid. But when she released me, I pulled her into me again, and indicated with the tenacity of my embrace that I'd like to hold her for at least a full minute or two, binge on her now, and thus be left sated. I was overcome: I coveted her and the world in that order.

I kept a close eye on the side of her head, to see if she would turn her face toward mine. If that were to happen I would kiss her for a short time and then stop, and then laugh it off, pretend that we were just being dopes. I would kiss her long enough to satisfy my curiosity about kissing her but briefly enough that I could dismiss the kiss—ha ha what a riot, couldn't matter less.

But it would always matter! I would always think of this time, of these hugs, of a kiss, should it come. I would catalog it and reference it frequently, and I hoped that in the short term gorging on this kind of platonic affection would prevent me from doing something more drastic later. Faced with a radiance like here, a clear air of rightness, it took so much work to avoid doing something wrong. We held each other for three minutes and then pulled away and I kissed her head while she stared into my neck.

We got back in the car.

It was 8 o'clock and underwater blue when we rolled over the bridge to the Isle of Skye. There was fog, a hazy condensation that cast everything in gray. We had a map, but it was much too vague and soon we were lost. There was a profound sort of quiet to the island, and I wanted nothing more than a small warm inn, with only one room left, no doubles, sorry—so we'd have to share a bed.

We stopped at a small bed and breakfast, with a sign saying "Mrs. MacIlvane's", to ask about a room. There were luminaria guiding visitors to the door, a huge and scarlet door, with a knocker in the center fashioned from antlers. A large pale woman, who looked so much like Terry Jones in drag that I almost laughed, opened the door. I wanted her to speak in a chirpy falsetto but her voice was surprisingly nuanced, smoky even.

Erin asked if she had any rooms, and I saw that the woman hadn't noticed Erin's missing arm. Erin had a way of standing, which she'd used—she told me later—the first time I'd met her. It was an undetectable three-quarter stance, giving people a bit more of her right shoulder than was customary.

While the woman was telling us her son was home and occupying the one available room, the man of the house, round and with a leftward brush of gray hair, came up behind her and kicked the back of her knee, throwing her balance off. She turned, slapped his shoulder and they both grinned, bashful and proud, at Erin and me.

"You'll have a bit of trouble finding a room tonight," the man said.

"A load of birders up this weekend," his wife said. "Someone said there were puffins here, so they're all in search."

"Are you birders?" the man asked.

"Yes," said Erin. "Completely."

"Well, I'm sorry about the room," the man said. Now he was starting to close the door. "We'd invite you in, but you'd be sharing our bed."

"And we don't do that anymore," the woman said, out of view, laughing. And the big scarlet door closed on us.

Driving aimlessly, we speculated about their sex life. At some point I said something to Erin about her possibly wanting to have a three-way with the older couple.

"Sounds like you wanna go bump in the night with Terry Jones and her husband."

I think that's what I said. It was a joke, but I delivered it wrong and it sounded nasty.

Erin said, with all the cheer available in the world: "No thanks. Not this time."

I asked her what she meant by that.

"Nothing."

"So you've had a threesome!"

She was quiet.

"Erin! You dog."

More quiet.

"Who with?"

Nothing.

"Tell me. You have to tell me."

A sigh. "It was nothing. It was weird. Forget it. You see any more places to stay? On the map? I don't want to have to go back to Kyleakin."

This exchange was itself a level of intimacy we'd never had. When we'd shared stories before, it had always been voluntary—titillating but unchallenging. Now I was pushing her and I felt we were very close.

"Tell me who! Another girl, or a couple or what?"

"I don't know. Just stop."

"Who were they? Anyone I know? I bet it was two guys!"

We were having such a good time. At the same time, I felt like I was sticking my head ever-deeper into an oven.

"It was nothing. It was weird."

My mouth dried and I pretended to keep smiling. Why do we pursue information that we know will never leave our heads? I was inviting a permanent, violent guest into my home. He would defecate on my bed. He would shred my clothes, light fires on the walls. I could see him walking up the driveway and I stood at the door, knowing that I'd be a fool to bring him inside. But still I opened the door.

"You know I won't stop until you tell me," I said, still trying to be jocular.

A fog threw itself over our car and Erin turned on the brights.

"Who was it?" I asked, knowing. Almost knowing, as my eyes adjusted to the dim light now between us.

"Where is this coming from?" she asked. "Why are you obsessing?"

She looked in the side-view mirror and then rolled down the window to readjust it. I already knew I was right.

"Tell me," I said, hushed.

She stopped the car and turned to me. "You're being an ass. I thought you knew."

* * *

"Let me drive," I said.

We both got out silently and passed in front of the car, steam rising from the hood, our faces in the headlights white and terrified.

I drove faster. She was execrable. They were villains, the three of them. Vermin in Dockers. And liars. I closed my eyes and no colors appeared.

The black road devoured our headlights. I wove left and right with the double lines; they toyed with me. I couldn't imagine a time when I'd want to talk to her or to them again. It was almost a relief.

"Tom."

I didn't answer. I've wanted to be in a war. Or a box. Somewhere where I would always know what to do.

I didn't want to be in Scotland. Just getting off of Skye would mean something, having that bay between us. I'd go to Muck or Eigg or Benbecula or Rhum. How was it that I'd known? Far before she'd given me a hint I knew. I decided that yes, I wished she'd lied. I didn't like her face anymore. It had reddened and dropped—she almost had jowls, didn't she? Who was this person? She was an animal.

Two flashes of white and a boom and something black and two eyes—we hit a living thing. Erin gasped quietly, and I immediately had the strangely satisfying thought that she was so cowed by her sins to stay silent during a car accident. She couldn't scream.

I stopped the car.

"A dog, I think," she said.

I backed up. In my side-view mirror, a black mound marred the road, resting precisely on the divider. The brake lights were not enough to illuminate it. I turned the car around to shine the headlights on it. It was not a dog. It was a sheep.

Its wool was black and its eyes were almost white but also gray and blue. They reflected the car's lights flatly. There was blood coming from its mouth. Its head was twisted. Oh God, said Erin.

There were two white sheep by the side of the road. They were speaking to the dead black sheep. They made tentative steps toward the middle, where the black one's body lay. They wanted the dead sheep to get up and get going.

Erin and I both said Oh my God, oh my God, look at that. I thought, for the first time in my life, that the known science of the world was going to be changed by something I had witnessed. This communication between sheep, this cognizance of mortality, was surely unaccounted for.

"Should we pick it up?" Erin asked.

I considered this.

"No. It's in the middle," I said. "It won't get hit any-more—it's not in anyone's way. We should leave it."

The two sheep looked toward the car and spoke to Erin and me. *How would you?* They brayed at the car. *Don't you have enough? You fucking monsters!*

"Oh God," Erin said, "now they're talking to us."

Both sheep stepped toward the car. Quickly they picked up speed and started jogging at us.

"They're really scaring me," Erin said.

I backed up. I backed up fifty yards. I stopped the car again and watched. One sheep was still talking to us and the other had turned again, had resumed talking to the broken black one.

We drove then, both of us now very awake. As we slowed through Portree, a small town of tall clapboard taverns and

inns, shops of woolen goods, I was half-broken but only when
I concentrated on it. *Fuck those people.* I moved my mouth
when I thought this, and then I smiled. Erin saw me smile
and she didn't smile in return because she knew why I was
smiling.

The hotel in Portree had been awarded too many stars—it
was well-made and charmless. Twelve different newspapers
fanned out on a heavily lacquered table in the drawing room,
a robust fire chewing its cereal in the corner, the ceilings were
vaulted and the beds canopied, but there was a sickly tint to
the lighting, the smell of rain and frustration coming from the
walls. The only softening touch was a cat, sleeping atop the
bar. It yawned at me, showing its plasticine teeth.

We got a suite with two rooms.

"Tom," she said as we stepped up the quiet stairs.

I didn't answer her.

In the suite I closed my half from hers with a white sliding door. I changed and jogged down the steps alone, determined to claim the dining room as my own. Around my table,
unspeaking couples were watching me and breathing into
their plates. I looked out the picture window. The moon's
reflection was sketched loosely with chalk on the black flat
bay. The silverware was too heavy.

I woke up to coughing. Erin stumbled into the bathroom to
do it but that only made it louder, slapping against the tiled
walls. The sun was just coming up. She blew her nose. I
opened the sliding doors in time to catch her emerging from
the bathroom, naked below her small T-shirt. With the bathroom door open, she was backlit in gold. She turned the light
off and was black again.

"Sorry," she said. "Go back to sleep."

I squinted at her. Her legs were thinner than I'd expected, softer. I thought of white glue.

"I feel like hell."

I was thrilled. God had acted quickly. Erin was transformed: yesterday strong and quick-moving, now frail and sour. She threw back a shot of Nyquil and passed out.

I slid the doors and slept until nine. I wanted to be gone, but I worried about what the hotel staff would think of me leaving my one-armed friend alone, sick, while I flitted about the island. I left and told the man at the desk that Erin was resting, not to disturb her.

It was mid-afternoon and wet but my head was clear. It was more difficult to be angry at Erin while she was asleep and I was driving, away and alone. I was at Kyleakin, the tiny town of intersection with mainland Scotland, and stopped before the bridge ready to take me back over. I could leave her. I had a change of clean clothes in the car. A small group of buildings to the right, a small castle's ruins just beyond.

I stopped at a hostel. Everyone in the common room was young and pretending to be poor except, to the left, in the cafeteria, a family of five, Russian, eating spaghetti while assembling a jigsaw puzzle.

At the counter, I asked about a boat.

"We have one rowboat."

The boat, laying on the gray shore of rocks and sticks, everywhere black seaweed like the hair of a hundred dead mermaids, was overturned and silver. I untied the knot, righted it and dragged it to the water. I pushed it in and jumped from a rock, trying to keep my feet dry. The water here would be brutal. The tip of my right foot came into the boat wet, but otherwise I had done it. I was in the boat and it was moving from the shore. I was shooting out into the bay in this borrowed boat and I was alone and could be going anywhere.

But the boat was facing the wrong way. All I could see was the shrinking of that beach and those buildings. For a rowboat passenger all was adventure, facing forward, but for the rower it was work, the shoveling of coal in the furnace-room. I rowed until the hostel was vague and the castle ruins were a smudge. The water was smooth and the rowing easy. I was heading into the ocean.

I'd never owned a boat but now felt I'd wasted so many years. I laughed and laughed at the simplicity of it all, this boat, this water. I couldn't believe how stupid it was. I could pinch all this between my thumb and forefinger.

I rowed for twenty minutes and then heard barking. I looked to the shore, for a dog running along the beach. But I saw no dogs. I turned around and found myself fifty feet from a pair of rock islands breaking the water's surface, parallel, black, each the size of a bus. One was barren, but the one beyond it, about a hundred feet farther, was being busily evacuated by at least forty seals, platoons of seals, all barking and flopping and diving to get away from something. But what?

Oh.

I turned the boat and rowed away from the rocks; I felt terrible for upsetting them. I rowed quickly so they would return. I was halfway back to the shore when they began jumping back aboard their rock.

I turned the boat around again, heading back toward the

seals. I wanted to see them, had to. This time I stayed low, rowing slowly, almost imperceptibly turning my head periodically to check my direction and the state of the seals. The seals were not acting in a uniform way. They wrestled. They barked, they leapt on each other. Some would dive into the water and others would appear, shooting from the ocean as if falling from holes in the sky. It annoyed me, exasperated me, all their movements, without sense, all their bumping into each other, their flesh rubbing and undulating, all their noise. I expected these animals to be orderly. Their bodies were sensical, their cells and veins were mathematical. Was not everything, on a cellular level, well-maintained, logical and unimproveable, like a honeycomb? At some point, though, up the developmental ladder the order is lost and there is this, the bouncing and barking, everything foul.

And my feet were wet. My ankles were wet. I looked down. The boat was sinking. It was only a few inches above the water, which was plowing cheerfully through a hole under my seat. I tried to row but the boat was done for, immovable. The hole was enormous.

To shore it was five hundred yards at least. I'd freeze before I made it. I realized with clarity that I might die here, and could think only of what the three of them would do the weekend of my funeral, reunited again. I left my pants and shoes and belt in the boat and jumped before I could guess at the shock to my chest. My arms flailed but soon found a rhythm and I swam for shore, the car keys in my mouth, the sun now gone and the wind coming in. I swam with a necessary fury. I swallowed the coldest water.

On the beach I rose and felt huge. The Russian children from the hostel saw me emerge and ran back inside. The world had tried to kill me but there were explosions within my chest and I'd won. I had reached shore and would soon be inside the car, heat heaving. I would change clothes and be new.

Driving back to the hotel I knew that Erin was just a human in this world—her foibles weren't worth being angry about. She couldn't control herself if she wanted to, and all I could do, as someone who was capable of survival in any circumstances, was to have charity for Erin. Like a rat, she would mate with whomever or whatever she shared a cage. I had no anger anymore. I wanted to embrace her, to forgive her, to stroke her like a pet.

I came home to Erin and wanted to celebrate. I entered her room as she was waking up and slithering to the bathroom to vomit. I watched her lower her head below the toilet's rim, heard the sound of water being poured into water. I needed contact. I wanted her to see me alive. I wanted to eat her vomit—anything to put my mouth on hers.

"You awake?" I asked.

She was kneeling in front of the toilet.

"Not for long. Can you excuse me for a second?" she said, closing the door slowly.

"Sorry," I said, and went back to my own room.

I watched Sky News at the bar and drank two drinks I'd never had before, both with whisky, which I'd always loathed but now felt was the only appropriate drink for someone like myself, someone who could save his own life. It was late in the afternoon when I checked on Erin again, sliding the doors and finding her dressed and looking almost normal.

"You're up."

"I am. I feel good."

"I just heard you in the bathroom."

"Yeah, but that was the last one. I'm empty. I feel good. I want to drive somewhere," she said.

We drove.

We had the windows open and everything smelled wet, every blade of grass promising blooms. The roadsides were fenced and the sheep stayed clear. We got out three or four times by the coast, walking on wet brown paths to look down to the gray sea far below, past the hillside sheep and small white homes.

The rain came. The wind was strong and the air was scratched in straight lines, sky to earth. We got out once, at Moonen Bay, to walk on the shore of a small beach of large round stones, and were soaked in minutes. She spoke.

"Thanks for being good, Tom."

I nodded. I shook, drenched. She knew nothing.

As the day went dark we found ourselves near the top of the island. I was driving and Erin was looking at the map. She had found a lighthouse she wanted to see before it got too dark.

At Loch Mor we walked down a spongy hill to a valley. The sun was dropping then dropped, leaving a sky of frilly reds. The moon appeared too soon. The valley sloped around a teardrop-shaped lake, pink with the bizarre fuchsia bursts of the late-coming sunset. Violet heather bruised the green weedy ground as we jumped down. This was a place conceived in a burst of emotion by a melancholy boy.

I grabbed Erin around the waist and picked her up, throwing her over my shoulder. Look at this place! I wanted to say, but I chose to be mute, to punish her, perhaps. I put her down and she jogged away from me.

I caught up with her as she leaned against a rock wall,

facing the teardrop lake. My eyes focused on a broken white rock cleaved with moss. Does the rock cleave, allowing the moss, or does the moss cleave the rock? She put her chin on my chest.

"This is nice," she said.

"Where's the lighthouse?" I asked.

"It must be beyond that."

She was pointing to a huge outcropping, forty feet high, the shape of an anvil turned on its side. We followed a path as it swung down and to the right, sloping into the valley. The lighthouse couldn't be seen. When the path leveled out we walked to a cliff—a drop of eighty feet to a rocky beach and a malevolent surf. The moon now was high enough to reflect on the lake in a nickly shimmer.

Where we expected the path to end and the ocean to begin, the path instead continued, down, through another smallish valley, at the end of which was the lighthouse, on what seemed to be the very blue-black edge of this world. Erin gasped. The lighthouse was not alone and small, but huge, and surrounded by a cluster of dark buildings. It looked like a penitentiary complex, with fences and guard towers.

"Let's go down," I said.

"You can go," she said. "I'll watch you from here."

"I won't go alone. But I really want to see it."

"Sorry," she said. "That's too Witch Mountain for me."

We turned and the wind swept into the valley, its motives suspect. We pushed against it and walked up the hill, toward the car. Erin's jacket had no zipper or buttons; she held it closed with her hand. I pointed to a cluster of sheep far to our right. In the dark wind they looked ghostly, conspiring. They knew about the one we killed.

"Let's run," Erin said.

We did, up the path, and reached a small supply shed and rested. I was hot with my own exertion, and out of the wind it was much warmer. Erin had her back and head against the building, heaving. The sign on the shed, now just above our heads, said BEWARE WINCH OVERHEAD WHILST IN USE.

I leaned into Erin. I held her very close, and then kissed her hair.

"Sorry," she said, speaking into my chest.

"For what?"

"The lighthouse was my idea."

"Don't say sorry."

"I am, though. I'm sorry in general," she said.

Her face was red and rough; she looked so cold. I leaned into her again, and rubbed her back with my searching hands. The cold and her thighs had aroused me, and I was dizzy with the wind.

"Turn around," I said.

She faced the shed, her back to me. I opened my coat and wrapped it around her, my arms joined at her stomach.

"Warmer?" I asked.

"Yes." She did a quick shake to indicate her coziness, pushing herself into me. I was already hard. I assume she noticed, because she stopped moving.

I brought my mouth down to her ear and licked the top. She made no sound. I tightened my grip around her stomach and pulled her closer, throbbing against her. All was soaring, my head gone like buckshot. She reached around and rubbed my lower back, while I took her whole ear into my mouth and breathed hotly into it. She bent her knees and turned to face me.

"No," I said, turning her around again. I pulled her pants down and then my own.

"What are you doing?" she asked.

"I'm so..."

I couldn't finish the sentence.

"What?" she breathed.

"I just want..." I was feeling around between her legs, searching for moisture. I plunged my finger in.

"Ah! That hurt."

"Sorry," I said.

I moved myself between her legs, passing just under her. It was warm, dry. I needed—

"Wait," she said.

"I can't," I said. I found my way in and pushed. My cheek pressed into the back of her neck, her smooth hair in my mouth. I lunged further. She spread her feet, her hand above her, palm flat against the shed. I stepped back, hands on her hips and found my way fully inside. I felt huge within; it was so close, everything was. Her skin, exposed, was cold.

I opened my eyes and looked around and there were three sheep, not twenty feet away, staring, motionless. The wind scraped at the two of us, very small in the valley. The sheep did not move.

I couldn't keep my eyes closed, couldn't stop watching the sheep watch us. I was out of breath, I was frozen, dizzy. Without finishing I felt finished. I slipped out of her and stepped back. I buttoned my pants and backed away, in the path of the wind. The nickly shimmer of the moon sat blankly, doing nothing.

"Sorry," I said.

Her back to me, she dragged her pants up over her thighs. "Don't be sorry. That would make it weirder."

"Oh shit," I said. "This is so bad."

"Don't say that," she said. "It's bad if we say it's bad. It's not bad. It's fine."

I wanted to help her with her pants but I knew she'd refuse. I wanted to sit down. I wanted to be cut to pieces and eaten.

"Erin."

She slid down against the wall and sat. She squinted at me.

"That hurt, Tom."

"I'm sorry."

"Fuck!" she said. "Fuck! Fuck! Fuck-fuck!"

"Sorry."

"That hurt."

"Sorry."

"You should have at least waited."

I wanted to throw myself over the anvil-shaped rock. Or I wanted to tell Erin that I wanted to throw myself over, so that she would feel for me, see my grief. We both sat for a minute, occasionally glancing at each other. I wanted to erase the road that had brought me to her.

I tried to touch her shoulder where her arm was missing. She brushed my hand to the ground.

"Shit," she said. "This whole fucking year."

In Erin's room there was a cat. I'd seen this cat, in the hotel lobby, stepping gingerly along the granite mantle over the fireplace. It was very small and wailed when we entered.

"It's hungry," Erin said.

I didn't agree. I thought the animal just wanted more than she deserved, that she was surely fed all the time, but I said nothing. I was glad that Erin was speaking to me.

Erin decided to go downstairs to get milk for the cat, and when she opened the door, the cat tried to leave with her. But Erin pushed it inside and closed the door.

We would feed the cat and love it, name it. I found food in

the small fridge under the TV. Cashews. I opened the can and tossed cashew fragments on the carpet. The cat pounced and her head pecked at the nuts; she was finished in seconds. I dropped her another handful and she ate those. The door opened and Erin walked in with a glass of perfect white milk. I had never been happier than when she walked in. I would not be sent away, not yet.

Hours later, the cat was asleep, and Erin lay next to it, her eyes half-closed. There was purring. I felt content. Why does it give so much comfort to be responsible for someone's sleep? We all—don't we?—want creatures sleeping in our homes while we walk about, turning off lights. I wanted this now. I touched Erin's soft head and she allowed me. She allowed me because she was tired. She seemed so profoundly tired. After Scotland I would not hear from her again.

As my fingers spidered through the strands of Erin's hair, the brightness outside took my eyes from the room. The moon was striped by the blinds but I could see its nickly shimmer on the bay. It looked like aluminum foil, when crumpled and then smoothed with a thumb or the back of a knife. It smiled, eyed me with an unwelcome knowingness, and began to speak.

YOUR MOTHER AND I

I TOLD YOU about that, didn't I? About when your mother and I moved the world to solar energy and windpower, to hydro, all that? I never told you that? Can you hand me that cheese? No, the other one, the cheddar, right. I really thought I told you about that. What is happening to my head?

Well, we have to take the credit, your mother and I, for reducing our dependence on oil and for beginning the Age of Wind and Sun. That was pretty awesome. That name wasn't ours, though. Your uncle Frank came up with that. He always wanted to be in a band and call it that, the Age of Wind and Sun, but he never learned guitar and couldn't sing. When he sang he *enunciated* too much, you know? He sang like he was trying to teach English to Turkish children. Turkish children with learning disabilities. It was really odd, his singing.

You're already done? Okay, here's the Monterey Jack. Just dump it in the bowl. All of it, right. It was all pretty simple, converting most of the nation's electricity. At a certain point everyone knew that we had to just suck it up and pay the

money—because holy crap, it really was expensive at first!—
to set up the cities to make their own power. All those solar
panels and windmills on the city buildings? They weren't
always there, you know. No, they weren't. Look at some pictures, honey. They just weren't. The roofs of these millions of
buildings weren't being used in any real way, so I said, Hey,
let's have the buildings themselves generate some or all of the
power they use, and it might look pretty good, to boot—
everyone loves windmills, right? Windmills are awesome. So
we started in Salt Lake City and went from there.

Oh hey, can you grate that one? Just take half of that block
of Muenster. Here's a bowl. Thanks. Then we do the cheddar.
Cheddar has to be next. After the cheddar, pecorino. Never the
other way around. Stay with me, hon. Jack, Muenster, cheddar, pecorino. It is. The only way.

Right after that was a period of much activity. Your
mother and I tended to do a big project like the power con-
version, and then follow it with a bunch of smaller, quicker
things. So we made all the roads red. You wouldn't remember
this—you weren't even born. We were all into roads then, so
we had most of them painted red, most of them, especially the
highways—a leathery red that looked good with just about
everything, with green things and blue skies and woods of
cedar and golden swamps and sugar-colored beaches. I think
we were right. You like them, right? They used to be grey,
the roads. Insane, right? Your mom thinks yellow would have
been good, too, an ochre but sweeter. Anyway, in the same
week, we got rid of school funding tied to local property
taxes—can you believe they used to pull that crap?—banned
bicycle shorts for everyone but professionals, and made everyone's hair shinier. That was us. Your mother and I.

That was right after our work with the lobbyists—I never

told you that, either? I must be losing my mind. I never men-
tioned the lobbyists, about when we had them all deported?
That part of it, the deportation, was your mother's idea. All I'd
said was, Hey, why not ban all lobbying? Or at least ban all
donations from lobbyists, and make them wear cowbells so
everyone would know they were coming? And then your dear
mom, who was, I think, a little tipsy at the time—we were at
a bar where they had a Zima special, and you know how your
mom loves her Zima—she said, How about, to make sure
those bastards don't come back to Washington, have them all
sent to Greenland? And wow, the idea just took off. People
loved it, and Greenland welcomed them warmly; they'd apparently been looking for ways to boost their tourism. They set up
some cages and a viewing area and it was a big hit.

So then we were all pumped up, to be honest. Wow, this
kind of thing, the lobbyists thing especially, boy, it really made
your mother horny. Matter of fact, I think you were conceived
around that time. She was like some kind of tsunam—

Oh don't give me that face. What? Did I cross some line?
Don't you want to know when your seed was planted? I would
think you'd want to know that kind of thing. Well then.
I stand corrected.

Anyway, we were on a roll, so we got rid of genocide. The
main idea was to create and maintain a military force of about
20,000 troops, under the auspices of the U.N., which could be
deployed quickly to any part of the world within about thirty-
six hours. This wouldn't be the usual blue helmets, watching
the slaughter. These guys would be badass. We were sick of the
civilized world sort of twiddling their thumbs while hundreds
of thousands of people killed each other in Rwanda, Bosnia,
way back in Armenia, on and on. Then the U.N. would send
twelve Belgian soldiers. Nice guys, but really, you have a geno-

cide raging in Rwanda, 800,000 dead in a month and you send *twelve Belgians*?

So we made this proposal, the U.N. went for it, and within a year the force was up and running. And man oh man, your mother was randy again. That's when your fecundation happened, and why we called you Johnna. I remember it now—I was wrong before. Your mother and I were actually caught in the U.N. bathroom, after the vote went our way. The place, all marble and brass, was full of people, and at the worst possible moment, Kofi himself walked in. He sure was surprised to see us in there, on the sink, but I have to say, he was pretty cool about it. He actually seemed to enjoy it, even watched for a minute, because there was no way we were gonna stop in the middle—

Fine. I won't do that again. It's just that it's part of the story, honey. Everything we did started with love, and ended with lust—

But you're right. That was inappropriate.

We went on a tear right after genocide, very busy. I attribute it partly to the vitamins we were on—very intense program of herbs and vitamins and protein shakes. We'd shoot out of bed and bounce around like bunnies. So that's when we covered Cleveland in ivy. You've seen pictures. We did that. Just said, Hey Cleveland, what if you were covered in ivy, all the buildings? Wouldn't that look cool, and be a big tourist attraction? And they said, "Sure." Not right away, though. You know who helped with that? Dennis Kucinich. I used to call him "Sparky," because he was such a feisty fella. Your mom, she called him "The Kooch."

We're gonna need all three kinds of salsa, hon. Yeah, use the small bowls. Just pour it right up to the edge. Right. Your brother likes to mix it up. Me, I'm a fan of the mild.

Right after Cleveland and the ivy we made all the kids memorize poetry again. We hadn't memorized any growing up—this was the seventies and eighties, and people hadn't taught that for years—and we really found we missed it. The girls were fine with the idea, and the boys caught on when they realized it would help them get older women into bed. Around that time we banned wearing fur outside of arctic regions, flooded the market with diamonds and gold and silver to the point where none had any value, fixed the ozone hole—I could show you that; we've got it on video—and then we did the thing with the llamas. What are you doing? Sour cream in the salsa? No, no. That's just wrong, sweetie. My god.

So yeah, we put llamas everywhere. That was us. We just liked looking at them, so we bred about six million and spread them around. They weren't there before, honey. No, they weren't. Oh man, there's one now, in the backyard. Isn't it a handsome thing? Now they're as common as squirrels or deer, and you have your mom and pop to thank for that.

It's jalapeño time. Use the smaller knife. You're gonna cut the crap out of your hand. You don't want one of these. You see this scar on my thumb? Looks like a scythe, right? I got that when we were negotiating the removal of the nation's bill-boards. I was climbing one of them, in Kentucky actually, to start a hunger strike kind of thing, sort of silly I guess, and cut the shipdoodle out of that left thumb.

Why the billboards? Have you even see one? In books? Well, I guess I just never really liked the look of them—they just seemed so ugly and such an intrusion on the collective involuntary consciousness, a blight on the land. Vermont had outlawed them and boy, what a difference that made. So your mother and I revived Lady Bird Johnson's campaign against them, and of course 98 percent of the public was with us, so the whole thing happened pretty quickly. We had most of the billboards down within a year. Right after that, your brother Sid was conceived, and it was about time I had my tubes tied.

Give me some of that cobbler, hon. We're gonna have the peach cobbler after the main event. I just wanna get the Cool Whip on it, then stick it in the freezer for a minute. That's Frank's trick. Frank's come up with a lot of good ideas for improving frozen and refrigerated desserts. No, that's not his job, honey. Frank doesn't have a job, per se.

I guess a lot of what we did—what made so much of this possible—was eliminate the bipolar nature of so much of what passed for debate in those days. So often the media would take even the most logical idea, like private funding for all sports stadiums or having all colleges require forty hours of commu- nity service to graduate, and make it seem like there were two equally powerful sides to the argument, which was so rarely the case. A logical fallacy, is what that is. So we just got them to keep things in perspective a bit, not make everyone so crazy, polarizing every last debate. I mean, there was a time when you couldn't get a lightbulb replaced because the press would find a way to quote the sole lunatic in the world who didn't want that lightbulb replaced. So we sat them all down, all the members of the media, and we said, "Listen, we all want to have progress, we all want a world for the grandkids and all. We know we're gonna need better gas mileage on the cars, and that all the toddlers are gonna need Head Start, and we're gonna need weekly parades through every town and city to keep morale up, and we'll have to get rid of Three Strikes and mandatory minimums and the execution of retarded prison- ers—and that it all has to happen sooner or later, so don't go blowing opposition to any of it out of proportion. Don't go getting everyone *inflamed*." Honestly, when lynchings were

originally outlawed, you can bet the newspapers made it seem
like there was some real validity to the pro-lynching side of
things. You can be sure that the third paragraph of any article
would have said "Not *everyone* is happy about the anti-lynching
legislation. We spoke to a local resident who is not at all happy
about it..." Anyway, we sat everyone down, served some car-
rots and onion dip and in a couple hours your mother and
I straightened all that out.

About then we had a real productive period. In about six
months, we established a global minimum wage, we made it
so smoke detectors could be turned off without having to rip
them from the ceiling, and we got Soros to buy the Amazon, to
preserve it. That was fun—he took us on his jet, beautiful
thing, appointed in the smoothest cherry and teak, and they
had the soda where you add the colored syrup yourself. You ever
have that kind? So good, but you can't overdo it—too much
syrup and you feel bloated for a week. Well, then we came
home, rested up for a few days, and then we found a cure for
Parkinson's. We did *so,* honey. Yes that was us. Don't you ever
look through the nice scrapbook we made? You should. It's in
the garage with your Uncle Frank. Are you sure he's asleep?
No, don't wake him up. Hell, I guess you have to wake him up
anyway, because he won't want to miss the *comida grande*.

After Parkinson's, we fixed AIDS pretty well. We didn't
cure it, but we made the inhibiting drugs available worldwide,
for free, as a condition of the drug companies being allowed to
operate in the U.S. Their profit margins were insane at the time,
so they relented, made amends, and it worked out fine. That was
about when we made all buildings curvier, and all cars boxier.

After AIDS and the curves, we did some work on elections.
First we made them no more than two months long, publicly
funded, and forced the networks to give two hours a night to

the campaigns. Around when you were born, the candidates
were spending about $200 million each on TV ads, because
the news wasn't covering the elections for more than 90 seconds a day. It was nuts! So we fixed that, and then we per-
fected online and phone voting. Man, participation went
through the roof. Everyone thought there was just all this apa-
thy, when the main problem was finding your damned polling
place! And all the red tape—register now, vote then, come to
this elementary school—but skip work to do it—on and on.
Voting on a Tuesday? Good lord. But the online voting, the
voting over the phone—man that was great, suddenly participation exploded, from about, what, 40 percent, to 88. We did
that over Columbus Day weekend, I think. I remember I'd
just had my hair cut very short. Yeah, like in the picture in the
hallway. We called that style the Timberlake.

And that's about when your mom got all kinky again. She
went out, bought this one device, it was kind of like a swing,
where there was this harness and—

Fine. You don't need to know that. But the harness figures
in, because that's when your mother had the idea—some of her
best ideas happened when she was lying down—to make it
illegal to have more than one president from the same imme-
diate family. That was just a personal gripe she had. We'd had
the Adamses and Bushes and we were about to have the
Clintons and your mother just got pissed. What the fuck? she
said. Are we gonna have a monarchy here or what? Are we that
stupid, that we have to go to the same well every time? This
isn't an Aaron Spelling casting call, this is the damned presi-
dency! I said What about the Kennedys? And she said Screw
'em! Or maybe she didn't say that, but that was the spirit of
it. She's a fiery one, your mom, a fiery furnace of—

Ahem. So yeah, she pushed that through, a constitutional

amendment.

That led to another busy period. One week, we made all the cars electric and put waterslides in every elementary school. We increased average life expectancy to 164, made it illegal to manufacture or wear Cosby sweaters, and made penises better looking—more streamlined, better coloring, less hair. People, you know, were real appreciative about that. And the last thing we did, which I know I've told you about, was the program where everyone can redo one year of their childhood. For $580, you could go back to the year of your choice, and do that one again. You're not allowed to change anything, do anything differently, but you get to be there again, live the whole year, with what you know now. Oh man, that was a good idea. Everyone loved it, and it made up for all the people who were pissed when we painted Kansas purple, every last inch of it. I did the period between ten-and-a-half and eleven-and-a-half. Fifth grade. Wow, that was sweet.

Speaking of ten-year-olds, here comes your brother. And Uncle Frank! We didn't have to wake you up! *Hola hermano, tios! Esta la noche de los nachos! Si, si.* And here's your mother, descending the stairs. With her hair up. This I was particularly proud of, when I convinced your mother to wear her hair up more often. When she first did it, a week before our wedding, I was breathless, I was lifted, I felt as if I'd met her twin, and oh how I was confused. Was I cheating on my beloved with this version of her, with that long neck exposed, the hair falling in helixes, kissing her clavicles? She assured me that I was not, and that's how we got married, with her hair up— that's how we did the walk with the music and the fanfare, everything yellow and white, side by side, long even strides, she and me, your mother and I.

NAVEED

STEPHANIE IS in her own bedroom, among her things, and in her bedroom is James, whom she knows through friends and who has perfect forearms. Tonight they found themselves the last two at a party for a friend, who is leaving the country to go to Bolivia to raise llamas, or perhaps coffee. They are now in her bedroom, Stephanie and James, because they like each other a great deal, especially tonight, when his forearms looked truly exceptional. But James is only in Stephanie's city for one more week, at which time he will leave for Oregon to live as a forest-fire watchman of some kind. The point is that together they have no future, but Stephanie badly wants to have sexual intercourse with James. But if she does, James will bring her total number of sexual partners up to thirteen, which is, she thinks, too many. Not too many for herself—for she regrets only two of the men in question, both named Robert, both with too much back-fat—but too many for whomever she finally marries. She can already hear the conversation, a year or five years hence, with the man of her future, whoever he may be—he too will have amazing forearms—when after much fumbling and guessing and suspecting, they finally agree to exchange information about past partners: numbers, names, frequency, locales. And she knows now that thirteen will seem excessive. She believes that even twelve, where she is now, seems too much, will likely scare off a man who is not very secure in himself. But thirteen is something else, with other, more sinister complications. Thirteen is a baker's dozen, and it is this phrase, "baker's dozen," which is the problem. She knows that she will marry a well-adjusted and self-secure man with a sense of humor, and a man with a sense of humor will hear the number thirteen and will, she can be certain, make a joke involving the phrase "baker's dozen." And though they both will laugh when the fiancé utters the phrase, and laugh some more as he conjures the image of actual bakers, in their white outfits and hats and powdered hands, lining up for a crack at Stephanie—ha ha ho ho!—both Stephanie and her beloved will be privately sickened by the image and the phrase at its root and it will thus be the beginning of a quick unraveling of their love and respect for one another. They will not recover from the thought of her and these many baking men, of her being covered in flour, or pushed around in dough, or the inevitable, it would seem, incorporation of a rolling pin. All of this leaves her no choice, for the sake of her future: She must sleep not only with James, but with whomever becomes handy next weekend. His name will be Naveed and he will, she realizes in a moment of lustful revelation, give her fourteen, not thirteen, and for fourteen there are no expressions involving bakers, none involving tradesmen of any kind.

NOTES FOR A STORY
OF A MAN WHO WILL NOT
DIE ALONE

AROUND 8,000 words.

Quick-moving. Simple language. No descriptions of rooms or furnishings.

The man is in his seventies. He's ~~spry~~, lucid.

Possible names: Anson. Or Basil. Greg.

He doesn't want to die alone.

More than that, he wants to die surrounded by as many people as possible. The story is about if and how he might achieve this.

Why does he want to be surrounded by so many people? Many reasons, fear of course being high among them. He likes people. He likes to meet people. On a day when he meets fifty people, as at a church mixer or when getting signatures on a petition, he's much happier than on days when he meets no one. He leaves the TV on when he goes to sleep. This is one image/motif that recurs throughout. Many of us leave the TV on when we go to sleep. Some of us do it only when in hotels. But why do we do it, why did we do it as kids? Why, when young, did we take the greatest comfort in falling asleep under the dinner table with guests all around? Or on the coarse couch while our family watched a movie? Because we don't want to ✶ be alone when we leave the waking world?

Story takes place in Memphis. Should incorporate that huge glass pyramid, the one by the river, under the bridge.

Basil.

Basil has a terminal illness. Bone cancer. But this story shouldn't be about a suicide. There must be a way that he knows that he'll die, and that he can arrange or try to arrange a death surrounded by thousands, without actually taking his own life.

It starts with his having the idea one day. Maybe he's had shadows of the notion for many years, but it crystallizes now, and he goes to tell his children and brother. He has one brother, a bit older than himself, and three kids: two girls, who are now in their fifties, whom he raised with his longtime wife, who died twenty years ago now. She was taller than him. She smelled of lilacs. She had vitiligo. He also has a son, much younger, about twenty-three, whose mother was much younger than Basil. It was an affair. She is now remarried and lives in Tokyo.

The two daughters are horrified by the idea. Ashamed. They have no idea what's wrong with their father. The sisters want their father to pass away at home. Maybe, periodically, he embarrassed them as they were growing up. He was a straightforward enough man—he was an OB-GYN, let's say—but he was eccentric. His clothes were messy, always stained somewhere. They and their mother were neater. He occasionally drank to excess, worked obsessively on a Model T he'd bought in high school, and was the one who would get up in a restaurant and sing "Happy Birthday" to one of them, booming. He drove an old Trans Am until he was sixty, when he switched to a more fuel-efficient Hyundai. For years, he has collected cacti.

His son, a year out of college and a forest ranger/firefighter, understands what his father is talking about. He was always very afraid of the dark, for example. On the other hand, he's a more solitary person than his father. He loves his patrols on Mount St. Helens—that's where he works—and while he's friendly and sociable, he needs much more time alone than does Basil. Does he have a beard? He does.

His name is Dennis. Or Daniel or Derek. He is enlisted to help his father with the project.

But what exactly is the project? They're not sure where to start.

Basil calls an old friend, Helen, who he dated in his twenties. For decades she's been a well-known organizer of events—galas, premieres, political rallies, debutante parties. She knows how to book a space and bring in a crowd. In appearance and attitude, she's a bit like Ann Richards. Basil and Helen haven't spoken in about twenty years, but they're still friends, lazy friends.

They get back in touch. He arrives one day at her office, knowing he should call first. But he loves surprising people— another thing that annoys his daughters. He is ushered into Helen's office and they look at each other and see something very similar there. It's said that people who look alike are sometimes attracted to each other, and this happens here. They look alike in some fundamental way not affected by their being both older—maybe they both have close-set eyes and freckles.

They embrace and she sits on a chair next to him and they hold hands—she holds his fingers. She is luminous, he thinks. He is crazy, she thinks. She agrees to help.

Derek comes back to Tennessee to help his father. He will stay until the end. He and his father and Helen gather one afternoon in Basil's backyard. Basil has three dogs who fight constantly. They come into the house with new wounds every other day. Still, they all sleep in his bedroom, together and peacefully.

Helen knows this business, the business of events, so she floats some ideas. During halftime at a football game? The University of Tennessee? A Memphis State basketball game? A minor-league baseball game? The problem would be that the people attending wouldn't all want to witness such a thing, and that would be unfair. Basil decides this, that he doesn't want to foist his death upon anyone. Attendance must be voluntary.

But there's something appealing about the distance, Derek says. Watching from the fifty-yard line of a football field, if Basil were in the center of that field, would be much more palatable than being in very close quarters. Derek has watched a firefighter friend of his stop breathing, in a pickup truck, after withstanding burns over most of his body. He was overwhelmed by how hard it was to watch the breaths stop, each one quieter, by half, than the last. It would be better, he insists, if there can be a comfortable remove.

They clarify what Basil wants: He wants hundreds if not thousands of people. He wants there to be distance if desired. He wants to be able to meet people. There should be an optional receiving line, where people can come to him and wish him well, touch his hand or shoulder. Much like at a wake, though this would be for a still-living person, which makes more sense, of course. A conversation between Derek and Basil:

DEREK: Do you want to limit the receiving line to people you know?

BASIL: No, no. Anyone.

DEREK: So complete strangers should be able to come up and say hello, goodbye?

BASIL: Yes.

DEREK: But people are strange. Many people are strange. Aren't you afraid there'd be some strange person out there?

BASIL: At a thing like this? It'll be self-selecting, don't you think? People are strange, but more than that, they're good. They're good first, then strange.

DEREK: I guess. But there'll be Goth types, I bet. And evangelicals.

Should there be any kind of entertainment? Helen wants to know this. An orchestra? The event could be a concert. The whole departure set to music. This idea is accepted by all as a good one. Maybe the music follows a certain cycle, birth to death, music nodding to all the stages between.

Basil now is attached to the idea of music. Nothing too loud, though. No crashing cymbals.

They briefly consider simply having an event where they open a stadium and invite the public to come and say goodbye to a man named Basil.

The story could be called "All Say Goodbye to a Man Named Basil."

Maybe they do a test run, at a smaller venue. They place an ad in the paper, with words like those above, and that's all. They wait and wait and only seven people show up, and all of them quickly leave when they see only Basil, Helen and Derek.

They are getting closer to a solution. They know that the event should be large, and there should be music and perhaps some dancing, if relatively slow. No crazy dancing, Basil says. But slow dancing, waltzing, that kind of thing would be nice.

Basil himself is not so good at articulating why he wants this to be so, but his son and his friend Helen, in convincing others to help or attend, become the explainers. One sample conversation, between Derek and the Russian-born conductor of the Memphis Symphony, which Derek is attempting to get to play the event:

> DEREK: I think he just really likes to be around people. Lots of people.
>
> NIKITA: So why doesn't he just shoot himself in the middle of a hockey game or something? Sorry, that's not funny, I guess.
>
> DEREK: He doesn't want to foist himself upon people. He wants their attendance to be voluntary. We were thinking it would be a concert, and you could conduct.
>
> NIKITA: It is almost Russian in its gruesomeness.
>
> DEREK: We hope it will be beautiful.
>
> NIKITA: There has not been a beautiful death in the history of mankind.

There is some talk about what kind of precedent all this sets. A conversation between Helen and her assistant:

> ASST: I think it's great, but what if everyone wanted to

do this? The country would be sending off everyone with parades and parties and concerts.

HELEN: There's nothing wrong with that. We already have Lifetime Achievement Awards—everyone gets one of those now. And besides, there aren't that many Basils out there. I think this is seen as very strange behavior, and there are few people my age who go in for this sort of thing. For most, just the family around is fine, if that.

ASST: Aren't there elephants who go away from everyone to die? They go find a quiet place?

HELEN: I think most elephants do that. Lots of animals do, I think. Cats. Rhinos.

ASST: But are there animals that do *this*, animals that want to pass away in the company of thousands? I don't think so.

There is some discussion about whether or not there should be food, and Basil decides that food is fine. Wine would be good, though he's against beer or liquor, which might make the crowd too boisterous. But wine would be mellowing, he decides. Red wine, a cash bar.

There was that story of the Roman, Petronius, who was Nero's party planner. He had to come up with a better event every night, had to make each one more elaborate, bizarre, unforgettable. The story goes that one night he placed a tub in the middle of the festivities, and put himself in the tub. He then slit his wrists, letting the blood drain slowly into the tub. Periodically he would wrap his wrists, temporarily stanching the bleeding, to talk to a guest or two. But slowly he did die at that party, for those people.

Basil knows this story, and wants to make sure his is not like that. Helen agrees, and brings up an interesting point: for this to work, to have any dignity—to allow dignity to Basil and those watching—it has to be about Basil, not the audience. There can't be any motives in watching outside of Basil's asking them to be there, and their wanting to be present for an important moment in a stranger's life. Much like people cheer for those passing in a parade, though they don't know them.

Basil can't decide if this should be a daytime or nighttime event. During the day, it would seem more open and festive and light, and he would be able to see people's faces, if he chose. But at night, it could certainly be more beautiful, with everyone holding candles and the stars above. Ultimately he decides to compromise: it will be dusk.

There is a rich and melancholy undercurrent between Basil and Helen. They haven't been in contact for many decades, but now find themselves having great fun together, making each other laugh—Helen laughs with her stomach, her shoulders, and her face runs crimson quickly—and marveling at the other's strength and will. It's unfortunate that they came together again while she was essentially helping him to die. There is some hint that they might have a brief fling, but they decide not to bother. Basil's bones feel hollow, seashells stitched together with wire. Instead they can only shake their heads about the fact that they might have had many years of happiness together, alas. She also collects cacti.

Basil's older brother is either very sharp and feisty, or has lost his lucidity and lives in a constant-care facility. Probably the latter.

Someone, one of the daughters, proposes that the death could be on closed-circuit TV, allowing anyone to see it (though limiting the potential for public humiliation). This idea is rejected. It's not about the number of eyes watching from afar, Basil and Derek explain, it's about being in the company of many, feeling their heat.

Interesting sidenote: Basil only has so long to live, but his longevity depends to a certain extent on a relatively low-impact existence. But when he starts running around, planning this, making phone calls and getting into his car to scout locations and meet with people, he's stuck in a paradox. His very planning for the event is taking days off his life, which means he needs to work even harder, because his final day keeps moving up.

At some point Basil should have some doubts about it. After the preparations have been made. Maybe in the middle of the planning. Better: he calls it off when it's seeming too difficult. They haven't had much success with the arrangements, and he feels awful that it's taken Derek and Helen so much time to even get this far. He calls it off and Helen and Derek are actually somewhat relieved. They'd believed in him, and in the project, but are relatively happy to move on. A quiet death is a good death. It can be beautiful that way.

But about a week later, while watching the induction of a new Filipino president, he gets inspired anew. He calls them, asking to begin again. Or better than that: he starts doing it himself, not wanting to bother them. Derek finds out when Basil collapses one day from exhaustion, while looking into renting the deck of an aircraft carrier.

More people begin to help out. Friends of Derek's and Helen's, neighbors, friends, acquaintances, strangers. They operate out of Helen's guest house or a barn on her land, and the whole enterprise begins to have the flavor and feel of a movement, something inspired and with its own unstoppable momentum. Of the newcomers there's a strange mix of people—hospice workers, young idealists, grey hippies with wild brittle hair, a few people who wish they'd done more for their own family members. These people are the most fervent.

Basil becomes attached to the idea that he will *walk* into the stadium, if it's indeed a stadium. For the purpose of argument, let's say it's a stadium, and Basil begins to feel that he shouldn't be wheeled in or driven in on an ambulance or on a golf cart. That, instead, he should walk in, and then assume a position on a couch. Not a bed. A divan would be best, Helen says.

When they go to get permissions from owners, administrators, councilmen, vendors and the like, some people immediately understand it, and others are aghast. This part could involve the police, and an injunction, and some religious organization that doesn't approve and tries to stop the entire thing. Then again, this shouldn't be that kind of story. We'll suspend our disbelief a bit, have it all go smoother than it might in real life. We only have eight thousand words.

In the end, he is in an unplanned place. There is a break in the story, and instead of the stadium we've pictured the entire time, it's something different—a riverside amphitheater for example. Or in the middle of a NASCAR track. He is spirited through a crowd, who all touch him. He feels the burn of every hand. Or he's parachuted into the venue, attached to a professional jumper. He dies on the way down. No. Back to the original idea: he walks in, in a procession, much like the Olympic athletes when they walk in during the opening ceremonies.

People applaud. The day has come. There are about four thousand there. It's the minor-league ballpark in the middle of Memphis. Helen has arranged to have all the advertisements covered in white cloth. Actually, everything is covered in white. She's gotten the local housepainters union to loan all of their unsplattered dropcloths. The ballpark is white like heaven. Basil is stunned.

He walks in and everyone cheers. He waves. He is with his son Derek. His daughters have come, but are in the stands, drinking heavily so the details, whatever elements might be unpleasant when recollected later, are less clear. The scene is stirring; goodwill is everywhere. Who are these people? Some have traveled from very far, out of curiosity. Most are from the area. Basil has delivered many babies in his life, thousands, and many hundreds of those babies are here now, grown up and wishing Basil well.

He sits on the divan; he is tired from the walk, the excitement. The music plays; the Russian conductor has been convinced, as has most of his orchestra, though absent are the woodwinds. They play a mixture of Brahms, Mozart, Lizst, Ellington, the Commodores, Sam Cooke. They play the theme from *Raiders of the Lost Ark*, a favorite of Basil's. The sun is fading. It takes almost two hours before he settles down, becomes accustomed to all the people around him. He sees individual faces, eyes and heads and little arms and hands that he can take with him. There is a teenaged girl, entirely clad in denim, who is nodding intensely, twisting her hips to a rhythm of her own. She is wearing makeup everywhere, and her flesh spills from below her shirt, and her large painted eyes close for long periods of time, when she is alive to music made by troubled people, and she is here to say goodbye to Basil.

There are periods when they all sing along to a given song, like "You Send Me." Helen, Basil's most true love, sits beside him and watches his contented face. She worries that he will not want to leave now. What have we done? she wonders. He is staring now at a group of men and women who have brought their babies. He loves babies and he'll want to stay forever now; this is bliss, how can he pass from this? She begins to see the point in dying alone, in cold spare rooms in hospitals in suburbs—these rooms would not be missed, making the transition so much easier...

But Helen's fears are unfounded. As she watches Basil, and Derek watches his father, and thousands watch the man who appears to be closing his eyes with pleasure, Basil finds himself reverberating from this world to the next, passing into sleep. He hears the music the people are making, their voices everywhere, talking about nothing, laughing at nothing, and he is ready.

ABOUT THE MAN
WHO BEGAN FLYING
AFTER MEETING HER

WHEN HE MET HER and they liked each other a great deal, he heard things better, and in his eyes the lines of the physical world were sharper than before. He was smarter, he was more aware, and he thought of new things to do with his days. He considered activities which before had been vaguely intriguing but which now seemed urgent, and which must, he thought, be done with his new companion. He wanted to fly in light-weight contraptions with her. He had always been intrigued by gliders, parachutes, ultralights and hangliders, and now he felt that this would be a facet of their new life: that they would be a couple that flew around on weekends and on vacations, in small aircraft. They would learn the terminology. They would join clubs. They would have a trailer of some kind, or a large van, in which to hold their new machines and supple wings folded, and they would drive to new places to see from above. The kind of flying that interested him was close to the ground—less than a thousand feet above Earth. He wanted to see things moving quickly below him, wanted to be able to

wave to people below, to see wildebeest run and to count dol-
phins streaming away from shore. He hoped this was the kind
of flying she'd want to do, too. He became so attached to the
idea of this person and this flying and this life entwined that
he was not sure what he would do if it did not become actual.
It was odd, though, he thought, that while the notion of this
flying was his, and he would be the driving force behind the
carrying out of this plan, he needed another person, this new
person in his world, to enable him to do it. He didn't want to
do this flying alone; he would rather not do it than do it without her. But if he asked her to fly with him, and she expressed
reservations, or was not inspired, would he stay with her?
Could he? He decides that he would not. If she does not drive
in the van with the wings carefully folded, he will have to
leave, smile and leave, and then he will look again. But when
and if he finds another companion, he knows his plan will not
be for flying. It will be another plan with another person,
because if he goes flying close to the Earth it will be with her.

UP THE MOUNTAIN COMING
DOWN SLOWLY

SHE LIES, SHE LIES, Rita lies on the bed, looking up, in the room that is so loud so early in Tanzania. She is in Moshi. She arrived the night before, in a Jeep driven by a man named Godwill. It is so bright this morning but was so madly, impossibly dark last night.

Her flight had arrived late, and customs was slow. There was a young American couple trying to clear a large box of soccer balls. For an orphanage, they said. The customs agent, in khaki head to toe, removed and bounced each ball on the clean reflective floor, as if inspecting the viability of each. Finally the American man was taken to a side room, and in a few minutes returned, rolling his eyes to his wife, rubbing his forefinger and thumb together in a way meaning money. The soccer balls were cleared, and the couple went on their way. Outside it was not humid, it was open and clear, the air cool and light, and Rita was greeted soundlessly by an old man, white-haired and thin and neat in shirtsleeves and a brown tie. He was Godwill, and he had been sent by the hotel to pick her up. It was midnight

and she was very awake as they drove and they had driven, on
the British side of the road, in silence through rural Tanzania,
just their headlights and the occasional jacaranda, and the constant long grass lining the way.

At the hotel she wanted a drink. She went to the hotel bar
alone, something she'd never done, and sat on a stool next to
a stenographer from Brussels. The stenographer, whose name
she did not catch and couldn't ask for again, wore a short inky
bob of black coarse hair and was wringing her napkin into tor-
tured shapes, tiny twisted mummies. The stenographer: face
curvy and shapeless like a child's, voice melodious, accent
soothing. They talked about capital punishment, the stenographer comparing the stonings common to some Muslim
regions with America's lethal injections and electric chairs.
Somehow the conversation was cheerful and relaxed. They had
both seen the same documentary about people who had witnessed executions, and had been amazed at how little it had
seemed to affect any of them, the watchers; they were sullen
and unmoved.

To witness a death! Rita could never do it. Even if they
made her sit there, behind the partition, she would close her
eyes and hum songs about candy.

Rita was tipsy and warm when she said good night to the
Brussels stenographer, who held her hand too long with her
cold slender fingers. Through the French doors and Rita was
outside, walking past the pool toward her mud hut, one of
twelve behind the hotel. She passed a man in a plain and green
uniform with a gun strapped to his back, an automatic rifle of
some kind, the barrel poking over his shoulder and in the dim
light seeming aimed at the base of his skull. She didn't know
why the man was there, and didn't know if he would shoot
her in the back when she walked past him, but she did, she

walked past him, because she trusted him, trusted this country and the hotel—that together they would know why it was necessary to have a heavily armed guard standing alone by the pool, still and clean, the surface dotted with leaves. She smiled at him and he did not smile back and she only felt safe again when she had closed the hut's door and closed the door to the tiny bathroom inside and was sitting on the cool toilet with her hands caressing her toes.

Morning comes like a scream through a pinhole. Rita is staring at the concentric circles of bamboo that comprise the hut's conical roof. She is lying still, hands crossed on her chest—she woke up that way—and through the mosquito net, too tight, terrifying, suffocating in a small way when she thinks too much about it, she can see the concentric circles of the roof above and the circles are twenty-two in number, because she has counted and recounted. She counted while lying awake, listening to someone, outside the hut, fill bucket after bucket with water.

Her name is Rita. Her hair is red like a Romanian's and her hands are large. Eyes large and mouth lipless and she hates, has always hated, her lipless mouth. As a girl she waited for her lips to appear, to fill out, but it never happened. Every year since her sixteenth birthday her lips have not grown but receded. The circles make up the roof but the circles never touch. Her father had been a pastor.

Last night she thought, intermittently, she knew why she was in Tanzania, in Moshi, at the base of Kilimanjaro. But this morning she has no clue. She knows she is supposed to begin hiking up the mountain today, in two hours, but now that she has come here, through Amsterdam and through the cool night

from the airport, sitting silently alone the whole drive, an hour
or so at midnight, next to Godwill—really his name was
Godwill, an old man who was sent by the hotel to pick her up,
and it made her so happy because Godwill was such a...
Tanzanian-sounding name—now that she has come here and is
awake she can not find the reason why she is here. She cannot
recall the source of her motivation to spend four days hiking up
this mountain, so blindingly white at the top—a hike some
had told her was brutalizing and often fatal and others had
claimed was actually just a walk in the park. She was not sure
she was fit enough, and was not sure she would not be bored to
insanity. She was most concerned about the altitude sickness.
The young were more susceptible, she'd heard, and at thirty-
eight she was not sure she was that anymore—young—but she
felt that for some reason she in particular was always susceptible and she would have to know when to turn back. If the pressure in her head became too great, she would have to turn back.
The mountain was almost twenty thousand feet high and every
month someone died of a cerebral edema and there were ways
to prevent this. Breathing deeply would bring more oxygen
into the blood, into the brain, and if that didn't work and the
pain persisted, there was Diamox, which thinned the blood and
accomplished the same objective but more quickly. But she
hated to take pills and had vowed not to use them, to simply
go down if the pain grew intolerable—but how would she
know when to go down? What were the phases before death?
She might at some point realize that it was time to turn and
walk down the mountain, but what if it was already too late?
It was possible that she would decide to leave, be ready to live
at a lower level again, but by then the mountain would have
had its way and there, on a path or in a tent, she would die.

She could stay in the hut. She could go to Zanzibar and

drink in the sun. She liked nothing better than to drink in the sun. With strangers. To drink in the sun! To feel the numbing of her tongue and limbs while her skin cooked slowly, and her feet dug deeper into the powdery sand! Drunk in the sun she felt communion with all people and knew they wished her the best.

Her hands are still crossed on her chest, and the filling of the buckets continues outside her hut, so loud, so constant. Is someone taking the water meant for her shower? At home, in St. Louis, her landlord with the beaver-fur coat was always taking her water—so why shouldn't it be the same here, in a hut in Moshi, with a gecko, almost translucent, darting across her conical ceiling, its ever-smaller circles never interlocking?

She has bought new boots, expensive, and has borrowed a backpack, huge, and a Therm-a-rest, and sleeping bag, and cup, and a dozen other things. Everything made of plastic and Gore-Tex. The items were light individually but together very heavy and all of it is packed in a large tall purple pack in the corner of the round hut and she doesn't want to carry the pack and wonders why she's come. She is not a mountain climber, and not an avid hiker, and not someone who needs to prove her fitness by hiking mountains and afterward casually mentioning it to friends and colleagues. She likes racquetball.

She has come because her younger sister, Gwen, had wanted to come, and they had bought the tickets together, thinking it would be the perfect trip to take before Gwen began making a family with her husband, Brad. But Gwen had gone ahead and gotten pregnant anyway, early, six months ahead of schedule and now she could not make the climb. She could not make the climb but that did not preclude—Gwen used the word liberally and randomly, like some use curry—her, Rita, from going. The trip was not refundable, so why not go?

Rita slides her hands from her chest to her thighs and holds them, her thin thighs, as if to steady them. Who is filling the bucket? She imagines it's someone from the shanty behind the hotel, stealing the hot water from the heater. She'd seen a bunch of teenage boys back there. Maybe they're stealing Rita's shower water. This country is so poor. Poorer than any place she's been. Is it poorer than Jamaica? She is not sure. Jamaica she expected to be like Florida, a healthy place benefiting from generations of heavy tourism and the constant and irrational flow of American money. But Jamaica was desperately poor almost everywhere and she understood nothing.

Maybe Tanzania is less poor. Around her hotel are shanties and also well-built homes with gardens and gates. There is a law here, Godwill had said in strained English, that all the men are required to have jobs. Maybe people chose to live in spartan simplicity. She doesn't know enough to judge one way or the other. The unemployed go to jail! Godwill had said, and seemed to like this law. He said this and then laughed and laughed.

In the morning widening quickly the sun is as clear and forthright as a spotlight and Rita wants to avoid walking past the men. She has already walked past the men twice and she has nothing to say to them. Soon the bus will come to take her and the others to the base of the mountain, and since finally leaving her bed she has been doing the necessary things—eating, packing, calling Gwen—and for each task she has had to walk from her hut to the hotel, has had to walk past the men sitting and standing along the steps into the lobby. Eight to ten of

them, young men, sitting, waiting without speaking. Godwill
had talked about this, that the men list their occupations as
guide, porter, salesperson, anything that will satisfy their government and didn't require them to be accounted for in one
constant place, because there really wasn't much work at all.
She had seen two of the men scuffle briefly over another
American's bag, for a one dollar tip. When Rita walked past
them she tried to smile faintly, without looking too friendly, or
rich, or sexy, or happy, or vulnerable, or guilty, or proud, or
contented, or healthy, or interested—she did not want them to
think she was any of those things. She walked by almost cross-
eyed with casual concentration.

Rita's face is wide and almost square, her jaw just short of
masculine. People have said she looks like a Kennedy, one of
the female Kennedys, the one on TV. But she is not beautiful
like that woman; she is instead almost plain, with or without
makeup, plain in any light. This she knows, though her friends
and Gwen tell her otherwise. She is unmarried and was for a
time a foster parent to siblings, a girl of nine and boy of seven,
malnourished by their birth mother, and Rita had contemplated adopting them herself—had thought her life through,
every year she imagined and planned with those kids, she
could definitely do it—but then Rita's mother and father had
beaten her to it. Her parents loved those kids, too, and had
oceans of time and plenty of room in their home, and there
were discussions and it had quickly been settled. There was a
long weekend they all spent together in the house where Rita
and Gwen were raised, Rita and her parents there with J.J. and
Frederick, the kids arranging their trophies in their new
rooms, and on Sunday evening, Rita said goodbye, and the
kids stayed there. It was easy and painless for everyone, and
Rita spent a week of vacation time in bed shaking.

Now, when she works two Saturdays a month and can't see them as often, Rita misses the two of them in a way that's too visceral. She misses having them both in her bed, the two little people, seven and nine years old, when the crickets were too loud and they were scared of them growing, the crickets, and of them together carrying away the house to devour it and everyone inside. This is a story they had heard, about the giant crickets carrying away the house, from their birth mother.

Rita is asleep on the bus but wakes up when the road inclines. The vehicle, white and square with rounded edges—it reminds her vaguely of something that would descend, backward, from a rocket ship and onto the moon—whinnies and shakes over the potholes of the muddy road and good Christ it's raining!—raining steadily on the way to the gate of Kilimanjaro. Godwill is driving and he's driving much too fast, and is not slowing down around tight curves, or for pedestrians carrying possessions on their heads, or for schoolchildren, who seem to be everywhere, in uniforms of white above and blue below. Disaster at every moment seems probable, but Rita is so tired she can't imagine raising an objection if the bus were sailing over a cliff.

"She's awake!" a man says. She looks to find Frank smiling at her, cheerful in an almost insane way. Maybe he is insane. Frank is the American guide, a sturdy and energetic man, from Oregon, medium-sized in every way, with a short-shorn blond beard that wraps his face as a bandage would a man, decades ago, suffering from a toothache. "We thought we'd have to carry you up. You're one of those people who can sleep through anything I bet." Then he laughs a shrill, girlish laugh, forced and mirthless.

They pass a large school, its sign posted along the road. The top half: Drive Refreshed: Coca-Cola; below: Marangu Sec. School. A group of women are walking on the roadside, babies in slings. The bus passes the Samange Social Club, which looks like a construction company trailer. Farther up the road, a small pink building, the K&J Hot Fashion Shop, bearing an enormous spray-painted rendering of Angela Bassett. A boy of six is leading a donkey. Two tiny girls in school uniforms are carrying a bag of potatoes. A driveway leads to the Tropical Pesticides Research Institute. The rain intensifies as they pass another school—Coca-Cola: Drive Refreshed; St Margaret's Catholic Sec School.

That morning, at the hotel, Rita had overheard a conversation between a British woman and the hotel concierge.

"There are so many Catholic schools!" the tourist had said. She'd just gotten back from a trip to a local waterfall.

"Are you Catholic?" the concierge had asked. The concierge was stout, with a clear nasal voice like a clarinet.

"I am," the tourist said. "And you?"

"Yes please. Did you see my town? Marangu?"

"I did. On the hill?"

"Yes please."

"It was very beautiful."

And the concierge had smiled.

The van passes a FEMA dispensary, a YMCA, another social club, called Millennium, a line of teenage girls in uniforms, plum-purple sweaters and skirts of sportcoat blue. They all wave. The rain is now real rain. The people they pass are soaked.

"Look at Patrick," Frank says, pointing at a handsome Tanzanian man on the bus, sitting across the aisle from him. "He's just sitting there smiling, wondering why the hell anyone would pay to be subjected to this."

Patrick smiles and nods and says nothing.

There are five paying hikers on the trip and they are introducing themselves. There are Mike and Jerry, a son and father in matching jackets. Mike is in his late twenties and his father is maybe sixty. Jerry has an accent that sounds British but possesses the round vowels of an Australian. Jerry owns a chain of restaurants, while the son is an automotive engineer, specializing in ambulances. They are tall men, barrel-chested and thin-legged, though Mike is heavier, with a loose paunch he carries with some effort. They wear matching red jackets, scarred everywhere with zippers, their initials embroidered on the left breast pockets. Mike is quiet and seems to be getting sick from the bus's jerking movements and constant turns. Jerry is smiling broadly, as if to make up for his son's reticence—a grin meant to introduce them both as happy and ready men, as gamers.

The rain continues, the cold unseasonable. There is a low fog that rises between the trees, giving the green a dead, faded look, as if most of the forest's color had drained into the soil.

"The rain should clear away in an hour or so," Frank announces, as the bus continues up the hills, bouncing through the mud. The foliage everywhere around is tangled and sloppy. "What do you think, Patrick?" Frank says. "This rain gonna burn off?"

Patrick hasn't spoken yet and now just shrugs and smiles. There is something in his eyes, Rita thinks, that is assessing. Assessing Frank, and the paying hikers, guessing at the possibility that he will make it up and down this mountain, this time, without losing his mind.

Grant is at the back of the bus, watching the land pass

through the windows, sitting in the middle of the bus's back-seat, like some kind of human rudder. He is shorter than the other two men but his legs are enormous, like a power lifter's, his calves thick and hairy. He is wearing cutoff jean shorts, though the temperature has everyone else adding layers. His hair is black and short-shorn, his eyes are small and water-cooler blue. He is watching the land pass through the window near his right cheek, and the wind waters his small calm eyes.

Shelly is in her late forties and looks precisely her age. She is slim, fit, almost wiry. Her hair, long, ponytailed, once blond, is fading to gray and she is not fighting it. She has the air of a lion, Rita thinks, though she doesn't know why she thinks of this animal, a lion, when she sees this small woman sitting two seats before her, in an anorak of the most lucid and expectant yellow. She watches Shelly tie a bandanna around her neck, quickly and with a certain offhand ferocity. Shelly's features are the features Rita would like for herself: a small thin nose with a flawless upward curve, her lips with the correct and volup-tuous lines, lips that must have been effortlessly sexual and life-giving as a younger woman.

"It's really miserable out there," Shelly says.

Rita nods.

"I'm finding myself annoyed by this," Shelly says.

Rita smiles.

The bus stops in front of a clapboard building, crooked, frowning, like a general store in a Western. There are signs and farm instruments attached to its side, and on the porch, out of the rain, there are two middle-aged women feeding fabric through sewing machines, side by side. Their eyes briefly sweep over the bus and its passengers, and then return to their work as the bus begins again.

Frank is talking about the porters. Porters, he says, will be accompanying the group, carrying the duffel bags, and the tents, and the tables to eat upon, and the food, and propane tanks, and coolers, and silverware, and water, among other things. Their group is five hikers and two guides, and there will be thirty-two porters coming along.

"I had no idea," Rita says to Grant, behind her. "I pictured a few guides and maybe two porters." She has a sudden vision of servants carrying kings aboard gilt thrones, elephants following, trumpets announcing their progress.

"That's nothing," Frank says. Frank has been listening to everyone's conversations and inserting himself when he sees fit. "Last time I did Everest, there were six of us and we had eighty Sherpas." He holds his hand horizontally, demonstrating the height of the Sherpas, which seems to be about four feet. "Little guys," he says, "but badasses. Tougher than these guys down here. No offense, Patrick."

Patrick isn't listening. The primary Tanzanian guide, he's in his early thirties and is dressed in new gear—a blueberry anorak, snowboarding pants, wraparound sunglasses. He's watching the side of the road, where a group of boys is keeping pace with the bus, each in a school uniform and each carrying what looks to be a small sickle. They run alongside, four of them, waving their sickles, yelling things Rita can't hear through the windows and over the whinnies of the van going up and up through the wet dirt. Their mouths are going, their eyes angry and their teeth are so small, but by the time Rita gets her window open to hear what they're saying the van is far beyond them, and they have run off the road with their sickles. They've dropped down the hillside, following some narrow path of their own making.

* * *

There is a wide black parking lot. MACHAME GATE reads a sign over the entrance. In the parking lot, about a hundred Tanzanian men are standing. They watch the bus enter the lot and park and immediately twenty of them converge upon it, unloading the backpacks and duffel bags from the bus. Before Rita and the rest of the hikers are off, all of the bags are stacked in a pile nearby, and the rain is falling upon them.

Rita is last off the bus, and when she arrives at the door, Godwill has closed it, not realizing she is still aboard.

"Sorry please," he says, yanking the lever, trying to get the door open again.

"Don't worry, I'm in no hurry," she says, giving him a little laugh.

She sees a man between the parking lot and the gate to the park, a man like the man at her hotel, in a plain green uniform, automatic rifle on his back.

"Is the gun for the animals, or the people?" she asks.

"People," Godwill says, with a small laugh. "People much more dangerous than animals!" Then he laughs and laughs and laughs.

It's about forty-five degrees, Rita guesses, though it could be fifty. And the rain. It's raining steadily, and the rain is cold. Rita hadn't thought about rain. When she had pictured the hike she had not thought about cold, cold, steady rain.

"Looks like we've got ourselves some rain," Frank says.

The paying hikers look at him.

"No two ways about it," he says.

Everything is moving rapidly. Bags are being grabbed, duffels hoisted. There are so many porters! Everyone is already wet. Patrick is talking with a group of the porters. They are dressed in bright colors, like the paying hikers, but their clothes—simple pants and sweatshirts—are already dirty, and their shoes are not large and complicated boots, as Rita is wearing, but instead sneakers, or track shoes, or loafers. None wear rain gear, but all wear hats.

Now there is animated discussion, and some pointing and shrugging. One porter jumps to the ground and then lies still, as if pretending to be dead. The men around him roar.

Rita ducks into her poncho and pulls it over her torso and backpack. The poncho was a piece of equipment the organizers listed as optional; no one, it seems, expected this rain. Now she is thrilled she bought it—$4.99 at Target on the way to the airport. She sees a few of the porters poking holes in garbage bags and fitting themselves within. Grant is doing the same. He catches Rita looking at him.

"Forgot the poncho," he says. "Can't believe I forgot the poncho."

"Sorry," she says. There is nothing else to say. He's going to get soaked.

"It's okay," he says. "Good enough for them, good enough for me."

Rita tightens the laces on her boots and readjusts her gaiters. She helps Shelly with her poncho, spreading it over her backpack, and arranges her hood around her leonine hair, frayed and thick, blond and white. As she pulls the plastic close to Shelly's face, they stare into each other's eyes and Rita has a sharp pain in her stomach, or her head, somewhere. She wants them here. They are her children and she allowed them to be taken. People were always quietly taking things from her, always with the understanding that everyone would be better off if Rita's life were kept simplified. But she was ready for complication, wasn't she? For a certain period of time, she was, she knows. It was the condominium that concerned everyone; she had almost bought one, in anticipation of adopting the kids, and she had backed out—but why?—just before closing. The place wasn't right; it wasn't big enough. She wanted it to be more right; she wanted to be more ready. It wasn't right, and the kids and her own parents would know it, and they would think she would always be insolvent, and they would always have to share a room. Gwen had offered to co-sign on the other place, the place they looked at with the yard and the three bedrooms, but that wouldn't be right, having Gwen on the mortgage. So she had given up and the kids were now in her old room, with her parents. She wants them walking next to her asking her advice. She wants to arrange their hoods around their faces, wants to pull the drawstrings so their faces shrink from view and stay dry. Shelly's face is old and lined and she grins at Rita and clears her throat.

"Thank you, hon," she says.

They are both waterproof now and the rain tick-ticks onto the plastic covering them everywhere. The paying hikers are standing in the parking lot in the rain.

"Porters have dropped out," says Frank, speaking to the group. "They gotta replace the porters who won't go up. It'll take a few minutes."

"Are there replacements close by?" Shelly asks.

"Probably get some younger guys," Frank says. "The younger guys are hungry."

"Like the B-team, right?" Jerry says. "We're getting the B-team!" He looks around for laughs but no one's wet cold face will smile. "Minor leaguers, right?" he says, then gives up.

It is much too late to go home now, Rita knows. Still, she can't suppress the thought of running all the way, ten miles or so, mostly downhill, back to the hotel, at which point she would—no matter what the cost—fly to warm and flat Zanzibar, to drink and drink until half-blind in the sun.

Nearby in the parking lot, Patrick seems to settle something with the man he's speaking to and approaches the group.

"Very wet," he says, with a grimace. "Long day."

The group is going to the peak, a four-day trip up, two down, along the Machame Route. There are at least five paths up the mountain, depending on what a hiker wants to see and how quickly they want to reach the top, and Gwen had promised that this route was within their abilities and by far the most scenic. The group's members each signed up through a website, EcoHeaven Tours, dedicated to adventure travel. The site promised small group tours of a dozen places—the Scottish highlands, the Indonesian lowlands, the rivers of upper Russia. The trip up this mountain was, oddly enough, the least exotic-sounding. Rita has never known anyone who had climbed Kilimanjaro, but she knew people who knew people who had, and this made it just that small bit less intriguing. Now, standing below the gate, this trip seems irrelevant, irrational, indefensible. She's walking the same way thousands have before, and she will be cold and wet while doing so.

"Okay, let's saddle up," Frank says, and begins to walk up a wide dirt path. Rita and the four others walk with him. Rita is glad, at least, to be moving, because moving will make her warm. They are all in ponchos, Grant in his garbage bag, all with backpacks beneath, resembling hunchbacks, or soldiers. She pictures the Korean War Memorial, all those young men, cast in bronze, eyes wide, waiting to be shot.

* * *

But Frank is walking very slowly. Rita is behind him; his pace is elephantine. Such measured movements, such lumbering effort. Frank is leading the five of them, with Patrick at the back of the group, and the porters are now distantly behind them, still in the parking lot, gathering the duffels and propane tanks and tents. They will catch up, Patrick said.

Rita is sure that this pace will drive her mad. She is a racquetball player because racquetball involves movement, and scoring, and noise, and the possibility of getting struck in the head with a ball moving at the speed of an airplane. And so she had worried that this hike would drive her mad with boredom. And now it is boring; here in Tanzania, she is bored. She will die of a crushing monotony before she even has a chance at a high-altitude cerebral edema.

After ten minutes, the group has traveled about two hundred yards, and it is time to stop. Mike is complaining of shoulder pain. His pack's straps need to be adjusted. Frank stops to help Mike, and while Frank is doing that, and Jerry and Shelly are waiting with Patrick, Grant continues up the trail. He does not stop. He goes around a bend in the path and he is out of view. The rain and the jungle make possible quick disappearances and before she knows why, Rita follows him.

She catches up to Grant and soon they are up two turns and can no longer see the group. Rita is elated. Grant walks quickly and she walks with him. They are almost running. They are moving at a pace she finds more fitting, an athletic pace, a pace appropriate for people who are not yet old. Rita is not yet old. She quit that 10k Fun Run last year but that didn't mean she couldn't have done it if it hadn't been so boring. She had started biking to work but then had decided against it; at the end of the day, when she'd done as much as she could before 5:30, she was just too tired.

They tramp through the mud and soon the path narrows and bends upward, more vertical, brushed by trees, the banana leaves huge, sloppy and serrated. The trail is soaked, the mud deep and grabbing, but everywhere the path is crosshatched with roots, and the roots become footholds. They jump from one root to the next and Grant is relentless. He does not stop. He does not use his hands to steady himself. He is the most balanced person Rita has ever known, and she quickly attributes this to his small stature and wide and powerful legs. He is close to the ground.

They talk very little. She knows he is a telephone-systems programmer of some kind, connects "groups of users" somehow. She knows he comes from Montana, and knows his voice is like an older man's, weaker than it should be, wheezy and prone to cracking. He is not handsome; his nose is almost piggish and his teeth are chipped in front, leaving a triangular gap, as if he'd tried to bite a tiny pyramid. He's not attractive in any kind of way she would call sexual, but she still wants to be with him and not the others.

The rainforest is dense and twisted and drenched. Mist obscures vision past twenty yards in any given direction. The rain comes down steadily, but the forest canopy slows and a hundred times redirects the water before it comes to Rita.

She is warmer now, sweating under her poncho and fleece, and she likes sweating and feels strong. Her pants, plastic pants she bought for nothing and used twice before while skiing, are loud, the legs scraping against each other with a constant, violent swipping sound. She wishes she were wearing shorts, like Grant. She wants to ask him to stop, so she can remove her pants, but worries he won't want to stop, and that anyway if he does and they do, the other hikers will catch up, and she and Grant will no longer be alone, ahead of the others, making good time. She says nothing.

There are no animals. Rita has not heard a bird or a monkey, or seen even a frog. There had been geckos in her hut, and larger lizards scurrying outside the hotel, but on this mountain there is nothing. Her guidebook had promised blue monkeys, colobus monkeys, galagos, olive baboons, bushbacks, duikers, hornbills, turacos. But the forest is quiet and vacant.

Now a porter is walking down the path, in jeans, a sweater, and tennis shoes. Rita and Grant stop and step to one side to allow him to pass.

"Jambo," Grant says.

"Jambo," the man says, and continues down the trail.

The exchange was quick but extraordinary. Grant had lowered his voice to a basso profundo, stretching the second syllable for a few seconds in an almost musical way. The porter had said the word back with identical inflection. It was like a greeting between teammates, doubles partners—simple, warm, understated but understood.

"What does that mean?" Rita asks. "Is that Swahili?"

"It is," Grant says, leaping over a puddle.

He says this in a polite way that nevertheless betrays his concern. Rita's face burns. She knows that Grant considers her a slothful and timid tourist. She wants Grant to like her, and to feel that she is more like him—quick, learned, seasoned— at least more so than the others, who are all so delicate, needy, and slow.

* * *

They walk upward in silence for an hour. The walking is med-
itative to an extent she thought impossible. Rita had worried
that she would either have to talk to the same few people—
people she did not know and might not like—for hundreds of
hours, or that, if the hikers were not so closely grouped, that
she would be alone, with no one to talk to, alone with her
thoughts. But already she knows that this will not be a problem. They have been hiking for two hours and she has not
thought of anything. Too much of her faculties have been
devoted to deciding where to step, where to place her left foot,
then her right, and her hands, which sometimes grip trees for
balance, sometimes touch the wet earth when a fall is likely.
The calculations necessary make unlikely almost any other
thinking—certainly nothing of any depth or complexity. And
for this she is grateful. It is expansive and well-fenced, her
landscape, the quiet acres of her mind, and with a soundtrack:
the tapping of the rain, the swipping of her poncho against the
branches, the tinny jangle of the carabiners swinging from her
backpack. All of it is musical in a minimal and calming way,
and she breathes in and out with an uncomplicated and
mechanical strength—plodding, powerful, robust.

"Poly poly," says a descending porter. He is wearing tasseled
loafers.

    "Poly poly," Grant says.

    "I got here a few days before the rest of you," Grant says, by
way of explanation and apology, once the porter has passed. He
feels that he's shamed Rita and has allowed her to suffer long
enough. "I spent some time in Moshi, picked up some things."

"'Jambo' is 'hello,'" he says. "'Poly poly' means 'step by step.'"

A porter comes up behind them.

"Jambo," he says.

"Jambo," Grant says, with the same inflection, the same stretching of the second syllable, as if delivering a sacred incantation. *Jaaaahmmmmboooow*. The porter smiles and continues up. He is carrying a propane tank above his head, and a large backpack sits between his shoulders, from which dangle two bags of potatoes. His load is easily eighty pounds.

He passes and Grant begins behind him. Rita asks Grant about his backpack, which is enormous, twice the size of hers, and contains poles and a pan and a bedroll. Rita had been told to pack only some food and a change of clothes, and to let the porters take the rest.

"I guess it is a little bigger," he says. His tone is almost too kind, too accommodating. It verges on the pedantic and Rita wonders if she'll hate the man in a matter of hours.

"Is that your tent in there, too?" she asks, talking to his back.

"It is," he says, stopping. He shakes out from under his pack and zippers open a compartment on the top.

"You're not having a porter carry it? How heavy is that thing?"

"Well, I guess... it's just a matter of choice, really. I'm... well, I guess I wanted to see if I could carry my own gear up. It's just a personal choice." He's sorry for carrying his things, sorry for knowing "hello." He spits a stream of brown liquid onto the ground.

"You dip?"

"I do. It's disgusting, isn't it?"

"You're not putting that sucker in there, too."

Grant is unwrapping a Charms lollipop.

"I'm afraid so. It's something I do. Want one?"

Rita wants something like the Charms lollipop, but now she can't separate the clean lollipops in his Ziploc bag—there are at least ten in there—from the one in his mouth, presumably covered in tobacco juice.

Minutes later, the trail turns and under a tree there is what looks like a hospital gurney crossed with a handcart. It's sturdy and wide, but with just two large wheels, set in the middle, on either side of a taut canvas cot. There are handles on the end, so it can be pulled like a rickshaw. Grant and Rita make shallow jokes about the contraption, about who might be coming down on that, but being near it any longer, because it's rusty and terrifying and looks like it's been used before and often, makes them think, and they don't want to think so they walk on.

When they arrive at a clearing, they've been hiking, quickly, for six hours. They are at what they assume to be their camp, and they are alone. The trees have cleared—they're now above treeline—and they're standing on a hillside, covered in fog, with high grass, thin like hair, everywhere. The rain has not subsided and the temperature has dropped. They have not seen any of the other hikers or guides for hours, nor have they seen any porters. Rita and Grant have been hiking quickly and beat everyone up the trail, and were not passed by anyone, and she feels so strong and proud about this. She can tell that in some way Grant is also proud, but she knows he wouldn't say so.

Within minutes she is shaking. It's no more than forty degrees and the rain is harder here; there are no trees diverting its impact. And there are no tents assembled, because they have beaten the porters to the camp. Even Grant seems to see the poor reasoning involved in their strategy. The one thing Grant doesn't have is a tarp, and without it there is no point in pitching his tent on earth this wet. They will have to wait, alone in the rain, until the porters arrive.

"It'll be at least an hour," Grant says.

"Maybe sooner for the porters?" Rita suggests.

"We sure didn't think this one through," he says, then spits a brown stream onto a clean green banana leaf.

Under a shrub no more than four feet tall, offering little protection, they sit together on a horizontal and wet log and let the rain come down on them. Rita tries not to shiver, because shivering is the first step, she remembers, to hypothermia. She slows her breathing, stills her body, and brings her arms from her sleeves and onto her naked skin.

Frank is furious. His eyes are wild. He feels compromised. The paying hikers are all in a cold canvas tent, sitting around a table no bigger than one meant for poker, and they are eating dinner—rice, plain noodles, potatoes, tea, orange slices.

"I know a few of you think you're hotshots," Frank says, blowing into his tea to cool it, "but this is no cakewalk up here. Today you're a speed demon, tomorrow you're sore and sick, full of blisters and malaria and God knows what."

Grant is looking straight at him, very serious, neither mocking nor confronting. He is staring at Frank as if Frank were explaining something on the menu.

"Or you get an aneurysm. There's a reason you have a guide, people. I've been up and down this mountain twelve times, and there's a reason for that." He blows into his tea again. "There's a reason for that."

He shakes his head as if suddenly chilled. "I need to know you're gonna act like adults, not like... yahoos!" And with that he burrows his thumb and forefinger into his eye sockets, a man with too much on his mind.

The food before the group has ostensibly been cooked, by the porters, but within the time it took to carry it from the tent where it was heated to this, their makeshift dining tent, the food has gone cold. Everyone eats what they can, though without cheer. The day was long and each hiker has an injury or an issue. Mike's stomach is already feeling wrong, and at some point Shelly slipped and cut her hand open on a jagged tree stump. Jerry is having the first twinges of an altitude headache. Only Rita and Grant are, for the time being, problem-free. Rita makes the mistake of announcing this, and it seems only to get Frank angrier.

"Well, it'll happen sooner or later, ma'am. Something will. You're probably better off being sick now, because in a few days, it'll hit you harder and deeper. So pray to get sick tonight, you two."

"You sit over there, you'll get dead," Jerry says, pointing to a corner of the tent where a hole is allowing a drizzle to pour onto the floor. "What kinda equipment you providing here anyway, Frank?" Jerry's tone is gregarious, but the message is plain.

"Are you dry?" Frank asks. Jerry nods. "Then you're fine."

They're sitting on small canvas folding stools, and the paying hikers have to hunch over to eat; there is no room for elbows. When they first sat down they had passed around and used the clear hand-sanitizing fluid provided—like Softsoap but cool and stinging lightly. Rita had rubbed her hands and tried to clear the dirt from her palms, but afterward found her hands no cleaner. She looks at her palms now, after two applications of the sanitizer, and though they're dry their every line and crevice is brown.

The man who brought the platters of rice and potatoes— named Steven—pokes his head into the tent again, his smile preceding him. He's in a purple fleece pullover with a matching stocking cap. He announces the coming of soup and everyone cheers. Soon there is soup finally and everyone devours it. The heat of the bodies of the paying hikers slowly warms the canvas tent and the candles on the table create the appearance of comfort. But they know that outside this tent the air is approaching freezing, and in the arc of night will dip below.

"Why are there no campfires?"

It's the first thing Mike has said at dinner.

"Honey collectors," Frank says. "Burned half the mountain."

Mike looks confused.

"They try to smoke out the bees to get the honey," Frank explains, "but it gets out of control. That's the theory anyway. Might have been a lot of things, but the mountain burned and now they won't allow fires."

"Also the firewood," Patrick says.

"Right, right," Frank says, nodding into his soup. "The porters were cutting down the trees for firewood. They were supposed to bring the firewood from below, but then they'd run out and start cutting whatever was handy. You're right, Patrick. I forgot about that. Now they're not even allowed to have firewood on the mountain. Illegal."

"So how do clothes get dry?" This from Jerry, who in the candlelight looks younger, and, Rita suddenly thinks, like a man who would be cast in a soap opera, as the patriarch of a powerful family. His hair is white and full, straight and smooth, riding away from his forehead like the back of a cresting wave.

"If there's sun tomorrow, they get dry," Frank says. "If there's no sun, they stay wet," he says, then sits back and waits for someone to complain. No one does, so he softens. "Put the wet clothes in your sleeping bag. Somewhere where you don't have to feel 'em. The heat in there will dry 'em out, usually. Otherwise work around the wet clothes till we get some sun."

"This is why those porters dropped out," Jerry says, with certainty.

"Listen," Frank says, "porters drop out all the time. Some of them are superstitious. Some just don't like rain. Doesn't mean a thing."

Rita cannot grip how this will work. She doesn't see how they can continue up the mountain, facing more rain, as it also becomes colder, the air thinner, and without their having any chance of drying the clothes that are surely too wet to wear. Is this not how people get sick or die? By getting wet and cold and staying wet and cold? Her concern, though, is a dull and almost distant one, because almost immediately after the plates are taken away, she feels exhausted beyond all measure. Her vision is blurry and her limbs tingle.

"I guess we're bunking together," Shelly says, suddenly behind her, above her. Everyone is standing up. Rita rises and follows Shelly outside, where it is still drizzling the coldest rain. The hikers all say goodnight, Mike and Jerry heading toward the toilet tent, just assembled—a triangular structure, three poles with a tarp wrapped around, a zipper for entry, and a three-foot hole dug below. Father and son are each carrying a small roll of toilet paper, protecting it from the rain with their plastic baggies containing their toothbrushes and paste. Their silhouettes are smudges scratched by the gray lines of the cold rain.

Shelly and Rita's tent is small and quickly becomes warm. Inside they crawl around, arranging their things, using their headlamps—a pair of miners looking for a lost contact lens.

"One day down," Shelly says.

Rita grunts her assent.

"Not much fun so far," Shelly says.

"No, not yet."

"But it's not supposed to be, I suppose. The point is getting up, right?"

"I guess."

"At all costs, right?"

"Right," Rita says, though she has no idea what Shelly is talking about.

Shelly soon settles into her sleeping bag, and turns toward Rita, closing her eyes. Shelly is asleep in seconds, and her breathing is loud. She breathes in through her nose and out through her nose, the exhalations in quick effortful bursts. Shelly is a yoga person and while Rita thought this was interesting an hour ago, now she hates yoga and everyone who might foster its dissemination.

The rain continues, tattering all night, almost rhythmic but not rhythmic enough, and Rita is awake for an hour, listening to Shelly's breathing and the rain, which comes in bursts, as if deposited by planes sweeping overhead. She worries that she will never sleep, and that she will be too tired tomorrow, that this will weaken her system and she will succumb to the cerebral edema that is ready, she knows, to leap. She sees the aneurysm in the form of a huge red troll, like a kewpie doll, the hair aflame, though with a pair of enormous scissors, like those used to open malls and car dealerships—

that the troll will jump from the mountain and with its great circus scissors sever Rita's medulla oblongata and her ties to this world.

Gwen is to blame. Gwen had wanted to help Rita do something great. Gwen had been ruthlessly supportive for decades now, sending money, making phone calls on Rita's behalf, setting her up with job interviews and divorced men who on the first date wanted to hold hands and their hands were rough and fat always, and Rita wanted no more of Gwen's help. Rita loved Gwen in an objective way, in an admiring way totally separate from her obligations to sibling affection. Gwen was so tall, so narrow, could not wear heels without looking like some kind of heron in black leggings, but her laugh was round and rolling, and it came out of her, as everything did, with its arms wide and embracing. She could be president if she'd wanted that job, but she hadn't— she'd chosen instead to torment Rita with her thoughtfulness. Baskets of cheese, thank-you notes, that long weekend in San Miguel when they'd rented the convertible Beetle. She even bought Rita a new mailbox and installed it, with cement and a shovel, when the old one was stolen in the night. This is what Gwen did, she did this and she humored Brad, and awaited her baby, and ran a small business, as fruitful as she could hope, that provided closet reorganization plans to very wealthy people in Santa Fe.

Rita knows she can't ask Shelly to share her sleeping bag but she wants a body close to her. She hasn't slept well since J.J. and Frederick went away because she has not been warm. No one ever said so but they didn't think it appropriate that the kids slept in her bed. Gwen had found it odd when Rita had bought a larger bed, but Rita knew that having those two bodies near her, never touching anywhere but a calf or ankle, her body calming their fears, was the only indispensible experience of her life or anyone else's.

As her heart blinks rapidly, Rita promises herself that the next day will be less punishing, less severe. The morning will be clear and dry and when the fog burns off, it will be so warm, maybe even hot, with the sun coming all over and drying their wet things. They will walk upward in the morning wearing shorts and sunglasses, upward toward the sun.

The morning is wet and foggy and there is no sun and everything that was wet the night before is now wetter. Rita's mood is a slashing despair; she does not want to leave her sleeping bag or her tent, she wants all these filthy people gone, wants her things dry and clean. She wants to be alone, for a few minutes at least. She knows she can't, because outside the tent are the other hikers, and there are twenty porters, and now a small group of German hikers and at the far side of the camp, three Canadians and a crew of twelve—they must have arrived after dark. Everyone is waking up. She hears the pouring of water, the rattle of pots, the thrufting of tents. Rita is so tired and so awake she comes close to crying. She wants to be in this sleeping bag, not awake but still sleeping, for two and a half hours more. In two and a half hours she could regather her strength, all of it. She would have a running start at this day, and could then leap past anyone.

There is conversation from the next tent. The voices are not whispering, not even attempting to whisper.

"You're kidding me," one voice says. "You know how much we paid for these tickets? How long did we plan to come here, how long did I save?"

It's Jerry.

"You know you didn't have to save, Dad."

"But Michael. We planned this for years. I talked to you about this when you were ten. Remember? When Uncle Mark came back? Christ!"

"Dad, I just—"

"And here you're going down after one freaking day!"

"Listen. I have never felt so weak, Dad. It's just so much harder than—"

"Michael. Yesterday was the hardest day—the rest will be nothing. You heard what's-his-face… Frank. This was the hard one. I can see why you're a little concerned, but you gotta buck up now, son. Yesterday was bad but—"

"Shhh."

"No one can hear us, Michael. For heaven's sake. Everyone's asleep."

"Shh!"

"I will not have you shushing me! And I won't have you—"

There is the sound of a sleeping bag being adjusted, and then the voices become lower and softer.

"I will not have you leaving this—"

And the voices dip below audibility.

Shelly is awake now, too. She has been listening, and gives Rita a raised eyebrow. Rita reciprocates, and begins searching through her duffel bag for what to wear today. She has brought three pairs of pants, two shorts, five shirts, two fleece sweatshirts, and her parka. Putting on her socks, wool and shaped like her foot, the ankle area reinforced and double-lined, she wonders if Mike will actually be going down so soon. There is a spare garbage bag into which she shoves her dirty socks, yesterday's shirt, and her jogging bra, which she can smell—rain and trees and a musty sweat.

"You'd have to break my leg," Shelly whispers. She is still

in her sleeping bag, only her face visible. Rita suddenly thinks she looks like someone. An actress. Jill Clayburgh. Jane Curtin? Kathleen Turner.

"Break my leg and cut my tendons. You'd have to. I'm doing this climb."

Rita nods and heads toward the tent's door flap.

"If you're going outside," Shelly says, "give me a weather report."

Rita pokes her head through the flaps and is facing fifteen porters. They are all standing in the fog, just across the campsite, under the drizzle, some holding cups, all in the clothes they were wearing yesterday. They are outside the cooking tent, and they are all staring at her face through the flap. She quickly pulls it back into the tent.

"What's it like?" Shelly asks.

"Same," Rita says, having never felt so sad.

Breakfast is porridge and tea and orange slices that have been left in the open air too long and are now dry, almost brown. There is toast, cold and hard and with hard butter needing to be applied with great force. Again the five paying hikers are hunched over the small card table, and they eat everything they can. They pass the brown sugar and dump it into their porridge, and they pass the milk for their coffee, and they worry that the caffeine will give them the runs and they'll have to make excessive trips to the toilet tent, which now everyone dreads. Rita had wondered if the trip might be too soft, too easy, but now, so soon after getting here, she knows that she is somewhere else. It's something very different.

"How was that tent of yours?" Frank asks, directing his chin toward Grant. "Not too warm, eh?"

"It was a little cool, you're right, Frank." Grant is pouring himself a third cup of tea.

"Grant thinks his dad's old canvas Army tent was the way to go," Frank says. "But he didn't count on this rain, didja, Grant? Your dad could dry his out next to the fire, but that ain't happening up here, friend."

Grant's hands are clasped in front of him, extending awkwardly, as if arm-wrestling with himself. He is listening and looking at Frank without any sort of emotion.

"That thing ain't dry tonight, you're gonna be bunking with me or someone else, my friend." Frank is scratching his beard in a way that looks painful. "Otherwise the rain and wind will make an icebox of that tent. You'll freeze in your sleep, and you won't even know it. You'll wake up dead."

The trail winds like a narrow river up through an hour of rainforest, drier today, and then cuts through a hillside cleared by fire. Everyone is walking together now, the ground bare and black. There are twisted remnants of trees straining from the soil, their extremities gone but their roots almost intact.

"There's your forest fire," Frank says.

The fog is finally clearing. Though the pace is slow, around a field of round rocks knee-high, it is not as slow as the day before, and because Rita is tired and her legs are sore in every place, from ankle to upper thigh, she accepts the reduced speed. Grant is behind her and also seems resigned.

But Mike is far more ill today. The five paying hikers know this because it has become the habit of all to monitor the health of everyone else. The question "How are you?" on this mountain is not rhetorical. The words in each case, from each hiker, give way to a distinct and complicated answer, involving the appearance or avoidance of blisters, of burgeoning headaches, of sore ankles and quads, shoulders that still, even with the straps adjusted, feel pinched. Mike's stomach feels, he is telling everyone, like there is actually a large tapeworm inside him. Its movements are trackable, relentless, he claims, and he's given it a name: Ashley, after an ex-girlfriend. He looks desperate for a moment of contentment; he looks like a sick child, lying on the bathroom floor, bent around the toilet, exhausted and defeated, who's forgotten what it was to feel strong.

Today the porters are passing the paying hikers. Every few minutes another goes by, or a group of them. The porters walk alone or in packs of three. When they come through they do one of two things: if there is room around the hikers, when the path is wide or there is space to walk through the dirt or rocks beside them, they will jog around them; when the path is narrow, they will wait for the hikers to step aside.

Rita and Grant are stepping aside.

"Jambo," Grant says.

"Jambo," the first porter says.

"Habari," Grant says.

"Imara," the porter says.

And he and the two others walk past. Rita asks Grant what he's just said. *Habari*, Grant explains, means How are you, and *imara* means strong. She watches them pass, noticing the last of the three. He is about twenty, wearing a CBS News T-shirt, khaki pants, and cream-colored Timberland hiking shoes, almost new. He is carrying two duffel bags on his head. One of them is Rita's. She almost tells the man this—Hey, that's my duffel you're carrying, ha ha!—this but then catches herself. There's nothing she can say in English she'd be proud of.

"Blue!" Jerry yells, pointing to a small spot of sky that the fog has left uncovered. It's the first swatch of blue the sky has allowed since the trip began, and it elicits an unnatural spasm of joy in Rita. She wants to climb through the gap and spread herself out above the cloudline, as you would a ladder leading to a treefort. Soon the blue hole grows and the sun, still obscured but now directly above, gives heat through a thin layer of cloudcover. The air around them warms almost immediately and Rita, along with the other paying hikers, stops to remove layers and put on sunglasses. Frank takes a pair of wet pants from his bag and ties them to a carabiner; they hang to his heels, filthy.

Mike now has the perpetual look of someone disarming a bomb. His forehead is never without sweat beaded along the ridges of the three distinct lines on his forehead. He is sucking on a silver tube, like a ketchup container but larger.

"Energy food," he explains.

They are all eating the snacks they've brought. Every day Steven gives the paying hikers a sack lunch of eggs and crackers, which no one eats. Rita is inhaling peanuts and raisins and chocolate. Jerry is gnawing on his beef jerky. They are all sharing food and needed articles of clothing and medical aid. Shelly loans Mike her Ace bandage, to wrap around his ankle, which he thinks is swollen. Jerry loans Rita a pair of Thinsulate gloves.

Fifteen porters pass while the paying hikers are eating and changing. One porter, more muscular than the others, who are uniformly thin, is carrying a radio playing American country music. The porter is affecting a nonchalant pride in this music, a certain casual ownership of it. To each porter Grant says jambo and most say jambo in return, eliciting more greetings from Jerry—who now likes to say the word, loudly.

"Jahm-BO!" he roars, in a way that seems intended to frighten.

Shelly steps over to Frank.

"What do the porters eat?" she asks.

"Eat? The porters? Well, they eat what you eat, pretty much," Frank says, then reaches for Shelly's hips and pats one. "Maybe without the snacking," he says, and winks.

There is a boom like a jet plane backfiring. Or artillery fire. Everyone looks up, then down the mountain. No one knows where to look. The porters, farther up the trail but still within view, stop briefly. Rita sees one mime the shooting of a rifle. Then they continue.

Now Rita is walking alone. She has talked to most of the paying hikers and feels caught up. She knows about Shelly's marriages, her unfinished Ph.D. in philosophy, her son living in a group home in Indiana after going off his medication and using a pizza cutter to threaten the life of a coworker. She knows Jerry, knows that Jerry feels his restaurants bring their communities together, knows that he fashioned them after Greek meeting places more than any contemporary dining model—he wants great ideas to be born over his food—and when he was expanding on the subject, gesturing with a stick he carried for three hours, she feared he would use the word *peripatetic*, and soon enough he did. She knew she would wince and she did. And she knows that Mike is unwell and is getting sicker and has begun to make jokes about how funny it would be for a designer of ambulances to lie dying on a mountain without any real way of getting to one.

The terrain is varied and Rita is happy; the route seems as if planned by hikers with short attention spans. There has been rainforest, then savannah, then more forest, then forest charred, and now the path cuts through a rocky hillside covered in ice-green groundcover, an ocean floor drained, the boulders everywhere huge and dripping with (lichen) of a seemingly synthetic orange.

The porters are passing her regularly now, not just the porters from her group but about a hundred more, from the Canadian camp, the German camp, other camps. She passes a tiny Japanese woman sitting on a round rock, flanked by a guide and a porter, waiting.

The porters are laboring more now. On the first day, they seemed almost cavalier, and walked so quickly that now she is surprised to see them straining, plodding and unamused. A small porter, older, approaches her back and she stops to allow him through.

"Jambo," she says.

"Jambo," he says.

He is carrying a large duffel with Jerry's name on it, atop his head, held there with the bag's thick strap, with cuts across his forehead. Below the strap, perspiration flows down the bridge of his nose.

"Habari?" she says.

"Imara," he says.

"Water?" she asks. He stops.

She removes her bottle from her backpack holster and holds it out to him. He stops and takes it, smiling. He takes a long drink from the wide mouth of the clear plastic container, and then continues walking.

"Wait!" she says, laughing. He is walking off with the water bottle. "Just a sip," she says, gesturing to him that she would like the container back. He stops and takes another drink, then hands it to her, bowing his head slightly while wiping his mouth with the back of his hand.

"Thank you," he says, and continues up the trail.

* * *

They have made camp. It's three in the afternoon and the fog has returned. It hangs lightly over the land, which is brown and wide and bare. The campground looks, with the fog, like a medieval battleground, desolate and ready to host the deaths of men.

Rita sits with Jerry on rocks the size and shape of beanbags while their tents are assembled. Mike is lying on the ground, on his backpack, and he looks to Rita much like what a new corpse would look like. Mike is almost blue, and is breathing in a hollow way that she hasn't heard before. His walking stick extends from his armpit in a way that looks like he's been lanced from behind.

"Oh Ashley!" he says to his tapeworm, or whatever it is. "Why are you doing this to me, Ashley?"

Far off into the mist, there is a song being sung. The words seem German, and soon they break apart into laughter. Closer to where she's sitting, Rita can hear an erratic and small sound, a tocking sound, punctuated periodically by low cheers.

The mist soon lifts and Rita sees Grant, who has already assembled his tent, surrounded by porters. He and a very young man, the youngest and thinnest she's seen, are playing a tennislike game, using thin wooden paddles to keep a small blue ball in the air. Grant is barefoot and is grinning.

"There he is," says Jerry. "Saint Grant of the porters!"

At dinner the food is the same—cold noodles, white rice, potatoes, but tonight instead of orange slices there is watermelon, sliced into neat thin triangles, small green boats with red sails on a silver round lake.

"Someone carried a watermelon up," Mike notes.

No one comments.

"Well, it didn't fly up," Frank says.

No one eats the watermelon, because the paying hikers have been instructed to avoid fruit, for fear of malaria in the water. Steven, the porter who serves the meals and whose smile precedes him always, soon returns and takes the watermelon back to the mess tent. He doesn't say a word.

"What happens to the guy who carried up the watermelon?" Jerry asks, grinning.

"Probably goes down," Frank says. "A lot of them are going down already—the guys who were carrying food that we've eaten. A lot of these guys you'll see one day and they're gone."

"Back to the banana fields," Jerry says.

Rita has been guessing at why Jerry looks familiar to her, and now she knows. He looks like a man she saw at Target, a portly man trying on robes who liked one so much he wore it around the store for almost an hour—she passed him twice. As with Jerry, she's both appalled by and in awe of their obliviousness to context, to taste.

The paying hikers talk about their dreams. They are all taking Malarone, an anti-malarial drug that for most fosters disturbing and hallucinatory dreams. Rita's attention wanes, because she's never interested in people's dreams and has had none of her own this trip.

Frank tells a story of a trip he took up Puncak Jaya, tallest peak in Indonesia, a mountain of 16,500 feet and very cold. They were looking for a climber who had died there in 1934, a British explorer who a dozen groups had tried to locate in the decades since. Frank's group, though, had the benefit of a journal kept by the climber's partner, recently found a few thousand feet below. Knowing the approximate route the explorer had taken, Frank's group found the man within fifteen minutes of reaching the correct elevation. "There he is," one of the climbers had said, without a trace of doubt, because the body was so well preserved that he looked precisely as he did in the last photograph of him. He'd fallen at least two hundred feet; his legs were broken but he had somehow survived, was trying to crawl when he'd frozen.

"And did you bury him?" Shelly asks.

"Bury him?" Frank says, with theatrical confusion. "How the heck we gonna bury the guy? It's eleven feet of snow there, and rock beneath that—"

"So you what—left him there?"

"Course we left him there! He's still there today, I bet in the same damned spot."

"So that's the way—"

"Yep, that's the way things are on the mountain."

Somewhere past midnight Rita's bladder makes demands. She tries to quietly extricate herself from the tent, though the sound of the inner zipper, and then the outer, is too loud. Rita knows Shelly is awake by the time her head makes its way outside of the tent.

Her breath is visible in compact gusts and in the air everything is blue. The moon is alive now and it has cast everything in blue. Everything is underwater but with impossible black shadows. Every rock has under it a black hole. Every tree has under it a black hole. She steps out of the tent and into the cold cold air. She jumps. There is a figure next to her, standing still.

"Rita," the figure says. "Sorry."

It's Grant. He is standing, arms crossed over his chest, facing the moon and also—now she sees it—the entire crest of Kilimanjaro. She gasps.

"It's incredible, isn't it?" he whispers.

"I had no idea—"

It's enormous. It's white-blue and huge and flat-topped. The clarity is startling. It is indeed blindingly white, even now, at 1 a.m. The moon gives its white top the look of china under candlelight. And it seems so close! It's a mountain but they're going to the top. Already they are almost halfway up its elevation and this fills Rita with a sense of clear unmitigated accomplishment. This cannot be taken away.

"The clouds just passed," Grant says. "I was brushing my teeth."

Rita looks out on the field of tents and sees other figures, alone and in pairs, also standing, facing the mountain.

Now she is determined to make it to its peak. It is very much, she thinks, like looking at the moon and knowing one could make it there, too. It is only time and breath that stand between her and the top. She is young. She'll do it and have done it.

She turns to Grant but he is gone.

Rita wakes up strong. She doesn't know why but she now feels, with her eyes opening quickly and her body rested, that she belongs on this mountain. She is ready to attack. She will run up the path today, barefoot. She will carry her own duffel. She will carry Shelly on her back. She has slept twice on this mountain but it seems like months. She feels sure that if she were left here alone, she would survive, would blend in like the hardiest of plants—her skin would turn ice-green and her feet would grow sturdy and gnarled, hard and crafty like roots.

She exits the tent and still the air is gray with mist, and everything is frozen—her boots covered in frost. The peak is no longer visible. She puts on her shoes and runs from the camp to pee. She decides en route that she will run until she finds the stream and there she will wash her hands. Now that this mountain is hers she can wash her hands in its streams, drink from them if she sees fit, live in its caves, run up its sheer rock faces.

It's fifteen minutes before she locates the stream. She was tracking and being led by the sound of the running water, without success, and finally just followed the striped shirt of a porter carrying two empty water containers.

"Jambo," she says to the man, in the precise way Grant does.

"Jambo," the porter repeats, and smiles at her.

He is young, probably the youngest porter she's seen, maybe eighteen. He has a scar bisecting his mouth, from just below his nose to just above the dimple on his chin. The containers are the size and shape of those used to carry gasoline. He lowers one under a small waterfall and it begins to fill, making precisely the same sound she heard from her bed, in her Moshi hut. She and the porter are crouching a few feet apart, his sweatshirt lashed with a zebra pattern in pink and black.

"You like zebras?" she asks. She rolls her eyes at her own inability to sound like anything but a moron.

He smiles and nods. She touches his sweatshirt and gives him a thumbs up. He smiles nervously.

She dips her hands into the water. Exactly the temperature she expected—cold but not bracing. She uses her fingernails to scrape the dirt from her palms, and with each trowel-like movement, she seems to free soil from her hand's lines. She then lets the water run over her palm, and her sense of accomplishment is great. Without soap she will clean these filthy hands! But when she is finished, when she has dried her hands on her shorts, they look exactly the same, filthy.

The sun has come through while she was staring at them, and she turns to face the sun, which is low but strong. The sun convinces her that she belongs here more than the other hikers, more than the porters. She is still not wearing socks! And now the sun is warming her, telling her not to worry that she cannot get her hands clean.

"Sun," she says to the porter, and smiles.

He nods while twisting the cap on the second container.

"What is your name?" she asks.

"Kassim," he says.

She asks him to spell it. He does. She tries to say it and he smiles.

"You think we're crazy to pay to hike up this hill?" she asks. She is nodding, hoping he will agree with her. He smiles and shakes his head, not understanding.

"Crazy?" Rita says, pointing to her chest. "To pay to hike up this hill?" She is walking her index and middle fingers up an imaginary mountain in the air. She points to the peak of Kilimanjaro, ringed by clouds, curved blades guarding the final thousand feet.

He doesn't understand, or pretends not to. Rita decides that Kassim is her favorite porter and that she'll give him her lunch. When they reach the bottom, she'll give him her boots. She glances at his feet, inside ancient faux-leather basketball shoes, and knows that his feet are much too big. Maybe he has kids. He can give the shoes to the kids. It occurs to Rita then that he's at work. That his family is at home while he is on the mountain. This is what she misses so much, coming home to those kids. The noise! They would just start in, a million things they had to talk about. She was interrupted all night until they fell asleep. They had no respect for her privacy and she loved them for their insouciance. She wants to sign more field trip permission slips. She wants to quietly curse their gym teacher for upsetting them. She wants to clean the gum out of J.J.'s backpack or wash Frederick's urine-soaked sheets.

Kassim finishes, his vessels full, and so he stands, waves goodbye, and jogs back to the camp.

In the sun the hikers and porters lay their wet clothes out on the rocks, hang them from the bare limbs of the trees. The temperature rises from freezing to sixty in an hour and everyone is delirious with warmth, with the idea of being dry, of everything being dry. The campsite, now visible for hundreds of yards, is wretched with people—maybe four hundred of them—and the things they're bringing up the mountain. There are colors ragged everywhere, dripping from the trees, bleeding into the earth. In every direction hikers are walking, toilet paper in hand, to find a private spot to deposit their waste.

Rita devours her porridge and she knows that she is feeling strong just as a few of the others are fading. They are cramped around the card table, in the tent, and the flaps are open for the first time during a meal, and it is now too warm, too sunny. Those facing the sun are wearing sunglasses.

"Lordy that feels good," Grant says.

"Thank God," Jerry says.

"You sure, dear Lord, we deserve this? Sure we haven't suffered enough?" Shelly says, and they laugh.

"I don't want to spoil the mood," Frank says, "but I have an announcement. I wanted to make clear that you're not allowed to give porters stuff. This morning, Mike thought it was a good idea to give a porter his sunglasses, and what happened, Mike?"

"Some other guy was wearing them."

"How long did it take before the sunglasses were on this other guy?"

"Fifteen minutes."

"Why's that, Mike?"

"Because you're supposed to give stuff to Patrick first."

"Right. Listen, people. There's a pecking order here, and Patrick knows the score. If you have a wave of generosity come over you and wanna give someone your lunch or your shoelaces or something, you give it to Patrick. He'll distribute whatever it is. That's the only way it's fair. That understood? You're here to walk and they're here to work."

Everyone nods.

"Why you giving your sunglasses away anyway, Mike? You're sure as hell gonna need 'em these next couple days. You get to the top and you're—"

"I'm going down," Mike says.

"What?"

"I have to go down," Mike says, staring at Frank, the sun lightening his blue eyes until they're sweater-gray, almost colorless. "I don't have the desire any more."

"The desire, eh?"

Frank pauses for a second, and seems to move, silently, from wanting to joke with Mike to wanting to talk him out of it to accepting the decision. It's clear he wants Jerry to say something, but Jerry is silent. Jerry will speak to Mike in private.

"Well," Frank says, "you know it when you know it, I guess. Patrick'll get a porter to walk you down."

Mike and Frank talk about how it will work. All the way down in one day? That's best, Frank says. That way you won't need provisions. Who brings my stuff? You carry your pack, a porter will carry the duffel. Get in by nightfall, probably, and Godwill will be there to meet you. Who's Godwill? The

driver. Oh, the older man. Yes. Godwill. He'll come up to get
you. If the park rangers think it's an emergency, they'll let him
drive about half the way up. So how much of a hike will we
make down? Six hours. I think I can do that. You can, Mike,
you can. You'll have to. No problem. Thanks for playing.
Better luck next time.

   Jerry still hasn't said anything. He is eating his porridge
quickly, listening. He is now chewing his porridge, his face
pinched, his eyes planning.

After breakfast Rita is walking to the toilet tent and passes the
cooking tent. There are six porters inside, and a small
tight group outside—younger porters, mostly, each holding a
small cup, standing around a large plastic tub, like those used
to bus dishes and silverware. Kassim is there; she recognizes
him immediately because he, like all of the porters, wears the
same clothes each day. There is another sweatshirt she knows,
with a white torso and orange sleeves, a florid Hello Kitty
logo on the chest. Rita tries to catch Kassim's eye but he's con-
centrating on the cooking tent. Steven steps through the flaps
with a silver bowl and overturns it into the tub. The young
porters descend upon it, stabbing their cups into the small
mound of porridge until it's gone in seconds.

The trail makes its way gradually upward and winds around
the mountain, and Mike, groaning with every leaden step, is
still with them. Rita doesn't know why he is still with the
group. He is lagging behind, with Patrick, and looks
stripped of all blood and hope. He is pale, and he is listing to
one side, and is using hiking poles as an elderly man would

use a cane, unsure and relying too heavily on that point at the end of a stick.

The clouds are following the group up the mountain. They should stay ahead of the clouds, Frank told them, if they want to keep warm today. There has been talk of more rain, but Frank and Patrick believe that it won't rain at the next camp—it's too high. They are hiking in a high desert area called the Saddle, between the peaks of Mawenzi, a mile away and jagged, and Kibo, above. The vegetation is now sparse, the trees long gone. Directly above the trail stands the mountain, though the peak is still obscured by cloud cover. She and Grant are still the only ones who have seen it, at midnight under the bright small moon.

Two hours into the day, Rita's head begins to throb. They are at 11,200 feet and the pain comes suddenly. It is at the back of her skull, where she was told the pain would begin and grow. She begins to breathe with more effort, trying to bring more oxygen into her blood, her brain. Her breathing works for small periods of time, the pain receding, though it comes back with ferocity. She breathes quickly, and loudly, and the pain moves away when she is walking faster, and climbing steeper, so she knows she must keep going up.

She walks with a trio of South Africans who have driven to Tanzania from Johannesburg. She asks them how long it took, the drive, and guesses at sixteen, eighteen hours. They laugh, no, no—three weeks, friend, they say. There are no superhighways in East Africa! they say. They walk along an easy path, a C-shape around the mountain, through a field of shale. The rocks are the color of rust and whales, shards that tinkle and clink, loudly, under their feet.

The path cuts through the most desolate side of Kilimanjaro, an area that looks like the volcano had spewed not lava but rusted steel. There is a windswept look about it, the slices of shale angled away from the mountaintop as if still trying to get away from the center, from the fire.

They descend into a valley, through a sparse forest of lobelia trees, all of them ridiculous-looking, each with the gray trunk of a coconut tree topped by an exuberant burst of green, a wild head of spiky verdant hair. A stream runs along the path, in a narrow and shallow crack in the valley wall, and they stop to fill their water bottles. The four of them squat like gargoyles and share a small vial of purification pills. They drop two of the pills, tiny and the color of steel, into the bottles and shake. They wait, still squatting, until the pills have dissolved, then they drop in small white tablets, meant to improve the water's taste. They stand.

She decides she will jog ahead of the South Africans, down the path. Weighing the appeal of learning more about the economic situation in sub-Saharan Africa against the prospect of running down this trail and making it to camp sooner, she chooses to run. She tells them she'll see them at the bottom and when she begins jogging, she immediately feels better. Her breathing is denser and her head clears within minutes. Exertion, she realizes, must be intense and constant.

There is a man lying in the path just ahead, as it bends under a thicket of lobelias. She runs faster, toward him. The body is crumpled as if it had been dropped. It's Mike. She is upon him and his skin is almost blue. He is asleep. He is lying on the path, his pack still strapped to his back. She dumps her pack and kneels beside him. He is breathing. His pulse seems slow but not desperate.

"Rita."

"You okay? What's wrong?"

"Tired. Sick. Ashley is killing me. Want to go home."

"Well, I'm sure you'll get your wish now. You're a mess."
He smiles.

Rita helps him stand and they walk slowly down the valley to the camp. It is spread out in a wide valley, the tents on the edge of a cliff—the camp this third day is stunning. It's late afternoon when they arrive and the sun is out and everywhere. This is the Great Barranco Valley, sitting high above the clouds, which lie like an ocean beyond the valley's mouth, as if being kept at bay behind glass.

The tents are assembled and she helps him inside one, his head on a pillow of clothes, the sun making the interior pink and alarming. When Jerry, already at camp and washing his socks in the stream, notices that his son is present, he enters the tent, asks Rita to leave, and when she does, zips the tent closed.

In her own tent Rita is wrecked. Now that she's not moving the pain in her head is a living thing. It is a rat-sized and prickly animal living, with great soaring breaths and a restless tail, in her frontal lobe. But there is no room for this animal in her frontal lobe, and thus there is great strain in her skull. The pain reaches to the corners of her eyes. At the corners of her brow someone is slowly pushing a pen or pencil, just behind her eyes and through, into the center of her head. When she places her first and second fingers on the base of her skull, she can feel a pulsing.

The tent is yellow. The sun makes the tent seem alive; she's inside a lemon. The air seems to be yellow, and everything that she knows about yellow is here—its glory and its anemia. It gets hotter, the sun reigning throughout the day, giving and giving, though with the heaviest heart.

The night goes cold. They are at 14,500 feet and the air is thin and when the sun disappears the wind is cruel, profane. The rain comes again. Frank and Patrick are amazed by the rain, because they say it is rare in this valley, but it begins just when the sun descends, a drizzle, and by dinner is steady. The temperature is plunging.

At dinner, tomorrow's hike—the final ascent—is mapped out. They will rise at 6 a.m., walk for eight hours, and stop at the high camp, where they'll eat and then sleep until 11 p.m. At 11, the group will get up, get packed, and make the final six-hour leg in the dark. They will reach the peak of Kibo at sunrise, take pictures, and dawdle for an hour before making the descent, eight hours to the final camp, halfway down the mountain, the path shooting through a different side this time, less scenic, quicker, straighter.

Shelly asks if all the porters go up with the group.

"What, up to the top? No, no," Frank says. About five do, just as guides, basically, he says. They come with the group, in case someone needs help with a pack or needs to go down. The rest of the porters stay at camp, then break it down and head out to meet the group at the final camp, on the long hike down.

After she's eaten, very little, Rita exits the tent and quickly bumps her head against the ear of a porter. It's the man with the water by the stream.

"Jambo," she says.

"Hello," he says. He is holding a small backpack. There are about twenty porters around the dining tent, though only three are carrying dishes away. With the tent empty, two more are breaking down the card table and chairs. The tent is soon empty and the porters begin filing in, intending, Rita assumes, to clean it before disassembling it.

Rita lies down. She lies down with great care and deliberation, resting her head so slowly onto the pillow Shelly has created for her from a garbage bag full of soft clothes. But even the small crinkling sound of the garbage bag is as loud as the collision of planets. Rita is scared. She sees the gravestone of the young man who died here six months before—they had a picture of it, and him—a beautiful young man grinning from below a blue bandanna—at the hotel, laminated on the front desk, to warn guests about pushing themselves too far. She sees her body being taken down by porters. Would they be careful with her corpse? She doesn't trust that they would be careful. They would want to get down quickly. They would carry her until they got to the rickshaw gurney and then they would run.

She listens as the paying hikers get ready for bed. She is in her sleeping bag and is still cold—she is wearing three layers but still she feels flayed. She shivers but the shivering hurts her head so she forces her body to rest; she pours her own calm over her skin, coating it as if with warm oil, and she breathes slower. Soon something is eating her legs. A panther is gnawing on her legs. She is watching the panther gnawing and can feel it, can feel it as if she were having her toes licked by a puppy, only there is blood, and bone, and marrow visible; the puppy is sucking the marrow from her bones, while looking up at her, smiling, asking What's your name? Do you like zebras?

* * *

She wakes up when she hears the rain growing louder. She shakes free of the dream and succeeds in forgetting it almost immediately. The rain overwhelms her mind. The rain is strong and hard, like the knocking of a door, the knocking getting louder, and it won't end, the knocking—sweet Jesus will someone please answer that knocking? She is freezing all night. She awakens every hour and puts on another article of clothing, until she can barely move. She briefly considers staying at this camp with the porters, not making the final climb. There are photographs. There is an IMAX movie. Maybe she will survive without summitting.

But she does not want to be grouped with Mike. She is better than Mike. There is a reason to finish this hike. She must finish it because Shelly is finishing it, and Grant is finishing it. She is as good as these people. She is tired of admitting that she cannot continue. For so many years she has been doing everything within her power to finish but again and again she has pulled up short, and has been content for having tried. She found comfort in the nuances between success and failure, between a goal finished, accomplished, and a goal adjusted.

She puts on another T-shirt and another pair of socks. She falls back to sleep. She wakes up in the dark, not long before dawn, and Shelly is holding her, spooning.

The light through the vent is like a crack into a world uninterrupted by shape or definition. There is only white. White against white. She squints and reaches for her sunglasses, reaches around to no avail, feels only the rocks beneath the tent. She is breathing as deeply as she can but it has no effect. She knows her head is not getting enough blood. Her faculties are slipping away. She tries to do simple mental tasks, testing

herself—the alphabet, states of the union, Latin conjuga-
tions—and finds her thoughts scattered. She inhales so deeply
the air feels coarse, and exhales with such force her chest goes
concave. Shelly is still asleep.

It's the first light of morning. If there is sun the rain must
have passed. It will not be so cold today—there is sun. Already
she is warmer, the tent heating quickly, but the wind is still
strong and the tent ripples loudly.

What is that? There is a commotion outside the tent. The
porters are yelling. She hears Frank, so close, unzip and rezip
his tent's door, and then can hear his steps move toward the
voices. The voices rise and fall on the wind, fractured by the
flapping of the tent.

There is someone trying to enter.

"Shelly," Rita says.

"Yes hon."

"Who is that?"

"That's me, dear."

Hours or seconds pass. Shelly is back. When did she leave?
Shelly has entered the tent, and is now slowly rezipping the
doorflap, trying not to bother her. Hours or seconds?

"Rita honey."

Rita wants to answer but can't find her tongue. The light
has swept into her, the light is filling her, like something liquid pushing its way into the corners of a mold, and soon she's
fading back to sleep. Hours or seconds?

"Rita honey, something's happened."

Rita is now riding on a horse, and she's on a battlefield of
some kind. She is riding sidesaddle, dodging bullets. She is
invincible, and her horse seems to be flying. She pats her horse
and the horse looks up at her, without warmth, bites her wrist
and keeps running, yanking on its reins.

Later she opens her eyes and it doesn't hurt. Something has changed. Her head is lighter, the pain is diminished. Shelly is gone. Rita doesn't know what time it is. It's still bright. Is it the same day? She doesn't know. Everyone could be gone. She has been left here.

She rises. She opens the tent door. There is a crowd around two men zipping up a large duffel bag. The zipper is stuck on something pink, fabric, a striped pattern. Now they have the duffel in the air, the bag connecting their left shoulders, and there are men around them arguing. Patrick is pushing someone away, and pointing the porters with the duffel down the path. Then there is another huge duffel, carried by two more porters, and they descend the trail. Grant is there. Grant is now helping lift a third duffel bag. He hoists his half onto his shoulder while another porter lifts the other side, and they begin walking, down the trail, away from the summit.

Rita closes her eyes again and flies off. There are bits of conversation that make their way into her head, through vents in her consciousness. "What were they wearing?" "Well, think about it like the cabbies again. It's a job, right? There are risks." "Are you bringing the peanuts, too?" "Sleeping through it all isn't going to make it go away, honey." "I don't have my headlamp. Does everyone else have a headlamp?"

J.J. and Frederick are in electric chairs. The Brussels stenographer is there, standing next to Rita, and they are smiling at the children. It is apparent in the logic of the dream that J.J. and Frederick are to be executed for losing a bet of some kind. Or because they were just born to be in the chair and Rita and the Brussels stenographer were born to hold their hands. J.J. and Frederick turn their eyes up to her. Rita is holding their hands as the vibrations start. She is resigned, knowing that there are rules and she is not the person to challenge them. But their teeth begin to chatter and their eyes rise to her and she wonders if she should do something to stop it.

"How do you feel, sweetie?"

Her head is clear and without weight. It again feels like part of her.

"You just needed time to acclimate, I bet." Shelly is stroking her leg.

Rita raises her head and there is no pain. Lifting her head is not difficult. She is amazed at the lightness of her head.

"Well, if you're coming, I think you'll have to be ready in a few minutes. We're already very late. We gotta get a move on."

Rita doesn't want to be in the tent anymore. She can finish this and have done it, whatever it is.

The terrain is rocky, loose with scree, and steep, but otherwise it is not the most difficult of hikes, she is told. They will simply go up until they are done. It will be something she can tell herself and others she has done, and being able to say yes when asked if she summitted will make a difference, will save her from explaining why she went down when two hikers over fifty years old went up.

Rita packs her parka and food, and stuffs the rest into her duffel bag for the porters to bring down to the next camp. The wind picks up and ripples the tent and she is struck quickly by panic. Something has happened. She remembers that Shelly had said something happened while she was asleep—but what? What was—

Mike. Oh Christ. Her stomach liquifies.

"Is Mike okay?" she asks.

She knows the answer will be no. She looks at Shelly's back.

"Mike? Mike's fine, hon. He's fine. I don't think he'll be joining us today, but he's feeling a little better."

Rita remembers Grant going down the trail. What happened to Grant?

"I'm sure we can find him at the bottom, afterward," Shelly says, applying a strip of white sunblock to her nose. "You can ask him then. He's not the most normal guy, though, is he?"

The sky is clear and though the air is still cold, maybe forty-five or so, the sun is warm to Rita's face. She is standing now, and almost can't believe she is standing. She steps over the shale to the meal tent, the thin shards of rock clinking like the closing of iron gates.

Mike is at breakfast. It's 8 a.m., and they are two hours behind schedule. They quickly eat a breakfast of porridge and hard-boiled eggs and tea. Everyone is exhausted and quiet. Grant has gone down the mountain and Mike is not going up. She smiles to Mike as he bites into an egg.

The remaining paying hikers—Rita, Jerry, Shelly—and Frank and Patrick say goodbye. They will see Mike again in about twelve hours, they say, and he'll feel better. They'll bring him some snow from Kibo, they say. They want to go and drag their bodies to the top, and from there they can look down to him.

It's glorious. From the peak Rita can see a hundred miles of Tanzania, green and extending until a low line of clouds intercepts and swallows the land. She can see Moshi, tiny windows reflecting the sun, like flecks of gold seen beneath a shallow stream. Everyone is taking pictures in front of a sign boasting the altitude at the top, and its status as the highest peak in Africa, the tallest freestanding mountain in the world. Behind the signs is the cavity of Kibo, a great volcanic crater, flat, paislied with snow.

On the Moshi side of the mountain, the glaciers are low and wide, white at the top and striped from her viewpoint, above. She sees the great teeth of a white whale. Icicles twenty feet tall extend down and drip onto the bare rock below.

"They're disappearing," Jerry says. He is standing behind Rita, looking through binoculars. "They melt every year a few feet. Coming down slowly but steadily. They'll be gone in twenty years."

Rita shields her eyes and looks where Jerry is looking.

There are others at the top of Kibo, a large group of Chinese hikers, all in their fifties, and a dozen Italians wearing light packs and with sleek black gear. The hikers who have made it here nod as they pass each other. They hand their cameras to strangers to take their pictures. The wind comes over the mountain in gusts, ghosts shooting over the crest.

The hike up had been slow and steep and savagely cold. They rested ten minutes every hour and while sitting or standing, eating granola and drinking water, their bodies cooled and the wind whipped them with broad sharp strokes. After four hours Shelly was faltering and said she would turn back. "Get that pack off!" Frank yelled, tearing it off her as if it were aflame. "Don't be a hero," he'd said, giving the pack to one of the porters. Shelly had continued, refreshed without the weight. The last five hundred yards, when they could see the tip of the mountain just above, had taken almost two hours. They'd reached the summit as the sun grew out of a band of violet clouds.

Now Rita is breathing as fast and as deeply as she can—her headache is fighting for dominion over her skull, and she is panting to keep it at bay. But she is happy that she walked up this mountain, and cannot believe she almost stopped before the peak. Now, she thinks, seeing these views in every direction, and knowing the communion with the others who have made it here, she would not have let anything stop her ascent. She knows now why a young man would continue up until crippled with edema, why his feet would have carried him while his head drained of blood and reason. Rita is proud of herself, and loves her companions, and now feels more connected to Shelly, and Jerry, Patrick, and Frank, than to Mike, or even Grant. Especially not to Grant, who chose to go down, though he was strong enough to make it. Grant is already blurry to her, someone she never really knew.

Rita finds Shelly, who is sitting on a small metal box chained to one of the signs.

"Well, I'm happy anyway," Shelly says. "I know I shouldn't be, but I am."

Rita sits next to her, panting to keep her head clear.

"Why shouldn't you be happy?" Rita asks.

"I feel guilty, I guess. Everyone does. But I just don't know how our quitting would have brought those porters back to life."

"Back to life? Who?"

"Last night," Shelly says. "Or the night before last. The last night we slept, when you were sick, Rita. Remember? The rain? It was so cold, and they were sleeping in the mess tent, and there was the hole, and the tent was so wet..."

"Why didn't we— Didn't someone—"

"They just didn't wake up, Rita. You didn't know? I know you were asleep but really, you didn't know? I think part of you knew. Who do you think they were carrying down?"

"I didn't see."

"They were young boys. They didn't have the right clothes. Can you imagine doing this without the right gear? Really, Rita? I thought maybe you knew. I think people have a sense for these things, when something like that is going on, don't you?"

"But why didn't we—"

"I didn't want to spoil all this for you. We've all worked so hard to get up here. I'm glad everyone decided to push through, because this is worth it, don't you think? Imagine coming all the way out here and not making it all the way up for whatever reason. Oh, look at the way the glaciers sort of radiate under the sun! They're so huge and still but they seem to pulse, don't they, honey? Look at the snow throbbing like that, pushing and pulling with us! Rita what— Where are you going?"

All the way down Rita expects to fall. The mountain is steep for the first hour, the rock everywhere loose. None of this was her idea. She was put here, in this place, by her sister, who was keeping score. Rita had never wanted this. Peaks mean nothing to her. She runs and then jumps and runs and then jumps, flying for twenty feet with each leap, and when she lands, hundreds of stones are unleashed and go rolling down, gathering more as they descend. She never would have come this far had she known it would be like this, all wrong, so cold and with the rain coming through the tents on those men. She makes it down to the high camp, where the porters made her dinner and went to sleep and did not wake up. This cannot be her fault. Patrick is responsible first, and Frank after him, and then Jerry and Shelly, both of whom are older, who have experience and should have known something was wrong. Rita is the last one who could be blamed; but then there is Grant, who had gone down and hadn't told her. Grant knew everything, didn't he? How could she be responsible for this kind of thing? Maybe she is not here now, running down this mountain, and was never here. This is something she can forget. She can be not-here—she was never here.

Yesterday she found herself wanting something she never wanted. To be able to tell Gwen that she'd done it, and she wanted to bring J.J. and Frederick a rock or something from up there, because then they'd think she was capable of anything finally and some day they would come back to her and—oh God she keeps running, sending scree down in front of her, throwing rocks down the mountain, because she cannot stop running and she cannot stop bringing the mountain down with her.

At the bottom, ten hours later, she is newly barefoot. The young boy who now has her boots, who she gave them to after he offered to wash them, directed her into a round hut of corrugated steel, and she ducked into its cool darkness. Behind a desk, flanked by maps, is a Tanzanian forest ranger. He is very serious.

"Did you make it to the top?" he asks.

She nods.

"Sign here."

He opens a log. He is turning the pages, looking for the last names entered. There are thousands of names in the book, with each name's nationality, age, and a place for comments. He finds a spot for her, on one of the last pages, at the bottom, and after all the names before her she adds her own.

THERE ARE SOME THINGS HE SHOULD KEEP TO HIMSELF

WHEN THEY LEARNED
TO YELP

THEY WERE OLDER than most when they learned to yelp. Most people, of most generations, in most of the world's nations, learn to yelp at a young age. Some are born yelping, others learn it when they learn their mother tongue. Yelping, as they say, comes with the territory. But these people, the ones we're talking about—born in the United States at a certain time— they had not learned to yelp.

"What is this you mean?" their friends abroad said. "This business about you have not yet learned to yelp? What is this, you are Canadian?"

To yelp: open your mouth. Convulse your stomach, as you would before a belch, or before vomiting. Now form a word, a thousand words, but emit none. In place of the words you might attempt, make a sound. The sound is a combination of three sounds. Each of these represents a third of your yelp.

First: there is the shrieking sound you might make if you

hit your head on the bottom edge of an open kitchen-cabinet door. It is sudden, high-pitched, angry. It speaks of the stupidity of pain.

Second: there is a whining aspect. Imagine that you have not slept for many days, and after those many days, you are punched in the gut. Then you are told to run over that hill yonder and back. When you return, you are punched in the sternum. You ask for mercy. They laugh and kill your dog. They break the objects you care about. This is the whine to keep in mind. This is exhaustion.

Third: the last factor in your yelp is the moan. The moan is the moan of powerlessless. The moan is shock in the face of natural horror. A landslide. An avalanche. Brutality. A flood. Machetes. This portion of your yelp says that you did not think you could be surprised or overwhelmed, but you have been proven wrong. You did not think, after seeing some ten thousand or so murders on television, after reading so much history, that anything could stick its fist through you. But you have been proven wrong. You did not want to be proven wrong.

When you combine these three things—the shriek, the whine, the moan—and condense them into a sharp burst that originates in your liver and expels itself from your body via all six to seven different orifices at once, you have yelped.

Yelping cannot be practiced or forced. Yelping will come only when provoked.

The yelp is efficient. The yelp says a great deal with great economy. The words, questions and statements which are encompassed in one quick yelp: Fuck! Shit! Piss! How could you? How could you? How do your hands do such things? I won't believe it. Stop it now. Please stop it now. Oh god. Oh god. Oh god. Motherfuckers! Animals! That poor man. Those poor women. Look at her arms. Look at his face. I cannot believe it. I will not believe it. Those bastards. Those mother-fucking bastards. This is not how it should be. Nothing should ever be like this. Goddamn all this. I give up. No, I will fight. No, I will give up. No, I will fight.

But for Americans of a certain age, there had until recently been no yelping. There were many of these words said, and emotions felt, and questions asked, but never had they been concentrated enough—for there must be an overwhelming onslaught of stimuli, gradual and topped off suddenly—to become a yelp. Their parents had yelped, most of them, and certainly their grandparents. But they had not, which made them at once stronger and less strong.

Those who have yelped have had their floor removed from them. The floor falls away and the yelper descends between 300 and 1500 feet, down a narrow shaft. Then the yelper must make his or her way back again, to the light.

Yelping can be done on cloudless days. Yelping can be done in any season. In any place. People yelped in beautiful Sarajevo. People yelped on the sugarwhite beaches of Haiti.

Yelping, though, can also be done—is very often done—far away from the source of its yelping. John Lundgren of Pittsfield, Massachusetts, reports having yelped while sitting in the bleachers at his niece's field hockey game; the man beside him had said, "Can you believe what happened?" and when

John heard what had happened, he yelped. Abby Peterson of Cliffside, Idaho, reports yelping while braiding her daughter's hair as they watched the news. She was stroking her daughter's smooth rust-colored strands when she saw something on the television and with her hands on her daughter's head she yelped. Chinaka Hodge of Oakland remembers being at the library, sitting at a white computer, the carpet beneath her quiet and blue. On the screen, when she sat down, was a short grainy film that she watched despite knowing that she should not watch it. And she yelped. She fell 720 feet and is now, many months later, still making her way back to the surface.

There had been some hope that these people would never know the sound we're talking about. That they would make it through their years without yelping. But now they and millions of others, Americans of a certain age, have followed the path of their parents and grandparents and billions of others before them. They have learned how to yelp. They cannot forget what it felt like—it burns, it burns—when the sound came out of them, but they can try to help those who have not yet yelped to live a yelping-free life. This is what we want. This is all that we can do.

AFTER I WAS THROWN
IN THE RIVER
AND BEFORE I DROWNED

OH I'M A FAST DOG. I'm fast-fast. It's true and I love being fast I admit it I love it. You know fast dogs. Dogs that just run by and you say, Damn! That's a fast dog! Well that's me. A fast dog. I'm a fast fast dog. *Hooooooo! Hooooooooooooo!*

You should watch me sometime. Just watch how fast I go when I'm going my fastest, when I've really got to move for something, when I'm really on my way—man do I get going sometimes, weaving like a missile, weaving like a missile between trees and around bushes and then *pop!* I can go over a fence or a baby or a rock or anything because I'm a fast fast dog and I can jump like a fucking gazelle.

Hooooooo! Man, oh man.

I love it I love it. I run to feel the cool air cool through my fur. I run to feel the cold water come from my eyes. I run to feel my jaw slacken and my tongue come loose and flap from the side of my mouth and I go and go and go my name is Steven.

I can eat pizza. I can eat chicken. I can eat yogurt and rye bread with caraway seeds. It really doesn't matter. They say No, no, don't eat that stuff, you, that stuff isn't for you, it's for us, for people! And I eat it anyway, I eat it with gusto, I eat the food and I feel good and I live on and run and run and look at the people and hear their stupid conversations coming from their slits for mouths and terrible eyes.

I see in the windows. I see what happens. I see the calm held-together moments and also the treachery and I run and run. You tell me it matters, what they all say. I have listened and long ago I stopped. Just tell me it matters and I will listen to you and I will want to be convinced. You tell me that what is said is making a difference, that those words are worthwhile words and mean something. I see what happens. I live with people who are German. They collect steins. They are good people. Their son is dead. I see what happens.

When I run I can turn like I'm magic or something. I can turn like there wasn't even a turn. I turn and I'm going so fast it's like I was still going straight. Through the trees like a missile, through the trees I love to run with my claws reaching and grabbing so quickly like I'm taking everything.

Damn, I'm so in love with all of this.

I was once in a river. I was thrown in a river when I was small. You just cannot know. I was swimming, trying to know why I had been thrown in the river. I was six months old, and my eyes were burning, the water was bad. I paddled and it was like begging. The land on either side was a black stripe, indifferent. I saw the gray water and then the darker water below and then my legs wouldn't work, were stuck in some kind of seaweed or spiderweb and then I was in the air.

I opened my burning eyes and saw him in yellow. The fisherman. I was lifted from the water, the water was below me. Then shivering on their white plastic boat bottom and they looked at me with their mustaches.

I dried in the sun. They brought me to the place with the cages and I yelled for days. Others were yelling too. Everyone was crazy. Then people and a car and I was new at home. Ate and slept and it was dry, walls of wood. Two people and two girls, thin twins who sleep in the next room, with a dollhouse between them.

When I go outside I run. I run from the cement past the places and then to where the places end and then to the woods. In the woods are the other dogs.

I am the fastest. Since Thomas left I am the fastest. I jump the farthest too. I don't have to yell anymore. I can go past the buildings where the people complain and then to the woods where I can't hear them and just run with these dogs. *Hoooooooooooooooooo!* I feel good here, feel strong. Sometimes I am a machine, moving so fast, a machine with everything working perfectly, my claws grabbing at the earth like I'm the one making it turn. Damn, yeah.

Every day on the street I pass the same people. There are the men, two of them, selling burritos from the steel van. They are happy men; their music is loud and jangles like a bracelet. There are the women from the drugstore outside on their break, smoking and laughing, shoulders shaking. There is the man who sleeps on the ground with the hole in his pants where his ass shows raw and barnacled and brown-blue. One arm extended, reaching toward the door of the building. He sleeps so much.

Every night I walk from the neighborhood and head to the woods and meet the others. It's shadowy out, the clouds low. I see the blues jumping inside the windows. I want all these people gone from the buildings and moved to the desert so we can fill the buildings with water. It's an idea I have. The buildings would be good if filled with water, or under water.

Something to clean them, anything. How long would it take to clean those buildings? Lord, no one knows any of this. So many of the sounds I hear I just can't stand. These people.

The only ones I like are the kids. I come to the kids and lick the kids. I run to them and push my nose into their stomachs. I don't want them to work. I want them to stay as they are and run with me, even though they're slow, so so slow. I run around them and around again as they run forward. They're slow but they are perfect things, almost perfect.

I pass the buildings. Inside, the women are putting strands of hair behind their ears, and their older children are standing before the mirror for hours, moving tentatively to their music. Their fathers are playing chess with their uncles who are staying with them for a month or so. They are happy that they are with each other, and I pass, my claws ticking on the sandpaper cement, past the man laying down with his arm reaching, and past the steel van with the music, and I see the light behind the rooftops.

I haven't been on a rooftop but was once in a plane and wondered why no one had told me. That clouds were more ravishing from above.

Where the buildings clear I sometimes see the train slip through the sharp black trees, all the green windows and the people inside in white shirts. I watch from the woods, the dirt in my nails so soft. I just cannot tell you how much I love all this, this train, these woods, the dirt, the smell of dogs nearby waiting to run.

In the woods we have races and we jump. We run from the entrance to the woods, where the trail starts, through the black-dark interior and out to the meadow and across the meadow and into the next woods, over the creek and then along the creek until the highway.

Tonight is cool, almost cold. There are no stars or clouds. We're all impotent but there is running. I jog down the trail and see the others. Six of them tonight—Edward, Franklin, Susan, Mary, Robert, and Victoria. When I see them I want to be in love with all of them at once. I want us all to be together; I feel so good to be near them. Some sort of marriage. We talk about it getting cooler. We talk about it being warm in these woods when we're close together. I know all these dogs but a few.

Tonight I race Edward. Edward is a bull terrier and he is fast and strong but his eyes want to win too much; he scares us. We don't know him well and he laughs too loud and only at his own jokes. He doesn't listen; he waits.

The course is a simple one. We run from the entrance through the black-dark interior and out to the meadow and across the meadow and into the next woods, along the creek, then the over the gap over the drainpipe and then along the creek until the highway.

The jump over the drainpipe is the hard part. We run along the creek and then the riverbank above it rises so we're ten, fifteen feet above the creek and then almost twenty. Then the bank is interrupted by a drainpipe, about four feet high, so the bank at eighteen feet has a twelve-foot gap and we have to run and jump to clear it. We have to feel strong to make it.

On the banks of the creek, near the drainpipe, on the dirt and in the weeds and on the branches of the rough gray trees are the squirrels. The squirrels have things to say; they talk before and after we jump. Sometimes while we're jumping they talk.

"He is running funny."

"She will not make it across."

When we land they say things.

"He did not land as well as I wanted him to."

"She made a bad landing. Because her landing was bad I am angry."

When we do not make it across the gap, and instead fall into the sandy bank, the squirrels say other things, their eyes full of glee.

"It makes me laugh that she did not make it across the gap."

"I am very happy that he fell and seems to be in pain."

I don't know why the squirrels watch us, or why they talk to us. They do not try to jump the gap. The running and jumping feels so good—even when we don't win or fall into the gap it feels so good when we run and jump—and when we are done the squirrels are talking to us, to each other in their small jittery voices.

We look at the squirrels and we wonder why they are there. We want them to run and jump with us but they do not. They sit and talk about the things we do. Sometimes one of the dogs, annoyed past tolerance, catches a squirrel in his mouth and crushes him. But then the next night they are back, all the squirrels, more of them. Always more.

Tonight I am to race Edward and I feel good. My eyes feel good, like I will see everything before I have to. I see colors like you hear jetplanes.

When we run on the side of the creek I feel strong and feel fast. There is room for both of us to run and I want to run along the creek, want to run alongside Edward and then jump. That's all I can see, the jump, the distance below us, the momentum taking me over the gap. Goddamn sometimes I only want this feeling to stay and last.

Tonight I run and Edward runs, and I see him pushing hard, and his claws grabbing, and it seems like we're both grabbing at the same thing, that we're both grabbing for the same thing. But we keep grabbing and grabbing and there is enough for both of us to grab, and after us there will be others who grab from this dirt on the creek bed and it will always be here.

Edward is nudging me as I run. Edward is pushing me, bumping into me. All I want is to run but he is yelling and bumping me, trying to bite me. All I want is to run and then jump. I am telling him that if we both just run and jump without bumping or biting we will run faster and jump farther. We will be stronger and do more beautiful things. He bites me and bumps me and yells things at me as we run. When we come to the bend he tries to bump me into the tree. I skid and then find my footing and keep running. I catch up to him quickly and because I am faster I catch him and overtake him and we are on the straightaway and I gain my speed, I muster it from everywhere, I attract the energy of everything living around me, it conducts through the soil through my claws while I grab and grab and I gain all the speed and then I see the gap. Two more strides and I jump.

You should do this sometime. I am a rocket. My time over the gap is a life. I am a cloud, so slow, for an instant I am a slow-moving cloud whose movement is elegant, cavalier, like sleep.

Then it speeds up and the leaves and black dirt come to me and I land and skid, my claws filling with soil and sand. I clear the gap by two feet and turn to see Edward jumping, and Edward's face looking across the gap, looking at my side of the gap, and his eyes still on the grass, exploding for it, and then he is falling, and only his front paws, claws, land above the bank. He yells something as he grabs, his eyes trying to pull the rest of him up, but he slides down the bank.

He is fine but in the past others have been hurt. One dog, Wolfgang, died here, years ago. The other dogs and I jump down to help Edward up. He is moaning but he is happy that we were running together and that he jumped.

The squirrels say things.

"That wasn't such a good jump."

"That was a terrible jump."

"He wasn't trying hard enough when he jumped."

"Bad landing."

"Awful landing."

"His bad landing makes me very angry."

I run the rest of the race alone. I finish and come back and watch the other races. I watch and like to watch them run and jump. We are lucky to have these legs and this ground, and that our muscles work with speed and the blood surges and that we can see everything.

After we all run we go home. A few of the dogs live on the other side of the highway, where there is more land. A few live my way, and we jog together back, through the woods and out of the entranceway and back to the streets and the buildings with the blue lights jumping inside. They know as I know. They see the men and women talking through the glass and saying nothing. They know that inside the children are pushing their toys across the wooden floors. And in their beds people are reaching for the covers, pulling, their feet kicking.

I scratch at the door and soon the door opens. Bare white legs under a red robe. Black hairs ooze from the white skin. I eat the food and go to the bedroom and wait for them to sleep. I sleep at the foot of the bed, over their feet, feeling the air from the just-open window roll in cool and familiar. In the next room the thin twins sleep alongside their dollhouse.

The next night I walk alone to the woods, my claws clicking on the sandpaper cement. The sleeping man sleeps near the door, his hands praying between his knees. I see a group of men singing on the corner drunkenly but they are perfect. Their voices join and burnish the air between them, freed and perfect from their old and drunken mouths. I sit and watch until they notice me.

"Get out of here, fuck-dog."

I see the buildings end and wait for the train through the branches. I wait and can almost hear the singing still. I wait and don't want to wait anymore but the longer I wait the more I expect the train to come. I see a crow bounce in front of me, his head pivoting, paranoid. Then the train sounds from the black thick part of the forest where it can't be seen, then comes into view, passing through the lighter woods, and it shoots through, the green squares glowing and inside the bodies with their white shirts. I try to soak myself in this. This I can't believe I deserve. I want to close my eyes to feel this more but then realize I shouldn't close my eyes. I keep my eyes open and watch and then the train is gone.

Tonight I race Susan. Susan is a retriever, a small one, fast and pretty with black eyes. We take off, through the entrance through the black-dark interior and out to the meadow. In the meadow we breathe the air and feel the light of the partial moon. We have sharp black shadows that spider through the long gray-green grass. We run and smile at each other because we both know how good this is. Maybe Susan is my sister.

Then the second forest approaches and we plunge like sex into the woods and take the turns, past the bend where Edward pushed me, and then along the creek. We are running together and are not really racing. We are wanting the other to run faster, better. We are watching each other in love with our movements and strength. Susan is maybe my mother.

Then the straightaway before the gap. Now we have to think about our own legs and muscles and timing before the jump. Susan looks at me and smiles again but looks tired. Two more strides and I jump and then am the slow cloud seeing the faces of my friends, the other strong dogs, then the hard ground rushes toward me and I land and hear her scream. I turn to see her face falling down the gap and run back to the gap. Robert and Victoria are down with her already. Her leg is broken and bleeding from the joint. She screams then wails, knowing everything already.

The squirrels are above and talking.

"Well, looks like she got what she deserved."

"That's what you get when you jump."

"If she were a better jumper this would not have happened."

Some of them laugh. Franklin is angry. He walks slowly to where they're sitting; they do not move. He grabs one in his jaws and crushes all its bones. Their voices are always talking but we forget they are so small, their head and bones so tiny. The rest run away. He tosses the squirrel's broken form into the slow water.

We go home. I jog to the buildings with Susan on my back. We pass the windows flickering blue and the men in the silver van with the jangly music. I take her home and scratch at her door until she is let in. I go home and see the thin twins with their dollhouse and I go to the room with the bed and fall asleep before they come.

* * *

The next night I don't want to go to the woods. I can't see someone fall, and can't hear the squirrels, and don't want Franklin to crush them in his jaws. I stay at home and I play with the twins in their pajamas. They put me on a pillowcase and pull me through the halls. I like the speed and they giggle. We make turns where I run into doorframes and they laugh. I run from them and then toward them and through their legs. They shriek, they love it. I want deeply for these twins and want them to leave and run with me. I stay with them tonight and then stay home for days. I stay away from the windows. It's warm in the house and I eat more and sit with them as they watch television. It rains for a week.

When I come to the woods again, after ten days away, Susan has lost her leg. The dogs are all there. Susan has three legs, a bandage around her front shoulder. Her smile is a new and more fragile thing. It's colder out and the wind is mean and searching. Mary says that the rain has made the creek swell and the current too fast. The gap over the drainpipe is wider now so we decide that we will not jump.

I race Franklin. Franklin is still angry about Susan's leg; neither of us can believe that things like that happen, that she has lost a leg and now when she smiles she looks like she's asking to die.

When we get to the straightaway I feel so strong that I know I will go. I'm not sure I can make it but I know I can go far, farther than I've jumped before, and I know how long it will be that I will be floating cloudlike. I want this. I want this so much, the floating.

I run and see the squirrels and their mouths are already forming the words they will say if I don't make it across. On the straightaway Franklin stops and yells to me that I should stop but it's just a few more strides and I've never felt so strong so I jump yes jump. I float for a long time and see it all. I see my bed and the faces of my friends and it seems like already they know.

When I hit my head it was obvious. I hit my head and had a moment when I could still see—I saw Susan's face, her eyes open huge, I saw some criss-crossing branches above me and then the current took me out and then I fell under the surface.

After I fell and was out of view the squirrels spoke.

"He should not have jumped that jump."

"He sure did look silly when he hit his head and slid into the water."

"He was a fool."

"Everything he ever did was worthless."

Franklin was angry and took five or six of them in his mouth, crushing them, tossing them one after the other. The other dogs watched; none of them knew if squirrel-killing made them happy or not.

After I died, so many things happened that I did not expect. The first was that I was there, inside my body, for a long time. I was at the bottom of the river, stuck in a thicket of sticks and logs, for six days. I was dead, but was still there, and I could see out of my eyes. I could move around inside my body like it was a warm loose bag. I would sleep in the warm loose bag, turn around in it like it was a small home of skin and fur. Every so often I could look through the bag's eyes to see what was outside, in the river. Through the dirty water I never saw much.

I had been thrown into the river, a different river, when I was young by a man because I would not fight. I was supposed to fight and he kicked me and slapped my head and tried to make me mean. I didn't know why he was kicking me, slapping. I wanted him to be happy. I wanted the squirrels to jump and be happy as we dogs were. But they were different than we were, and the man who threw me to the river was also different. I thought we were all the same but as I was inside my dead body and looking into the murky river bottom I knew that some are wanting to run and some are afraid to run and maybe they are broken and are angry for it.

I slept in my broken sack of a body at the bottom of the river, and wondered what would happen. It was dark inside, and musty, and the air was hard to draw. I sang to myself.

After the sixth day I woke up and it was bright. I knew I was back. I was no longer inside a loose sack but was now inhabiting a body like my own, from before; I was the same. I stood and was in a wide field of buttercups. I could smell their smell and walked through them, my eyes at the level of the yellow, a wide blur of a line of yellow. I was heavy-headed from the gorgeousness of the yellow all blurry. I loved breathing this way again, and seeing everything.

I should say that it's very much the same here as there. There are more hills, and more waterfalls, and things are cleaner. I like it. Each day I walk for a long time, and I don't have to walk back. I can walk and walk, and when I am tired I can sleep. When I wake up, I can keep walking and I never miss where I started and have no home.

I haven't seen anyone yet. I don't miss the cement like sandpaper on my feet, or the buildings with the sleeping men reaching. I sometimes miss the other dogs and the running.

The one big surprise is that as it turns out, God is the sun. It makes sense, if you think about it. Why we didn't see it sooner I cannot say. Every day the sun was right there burning, our and other planets hovering around it, always apologizing,

and we didn't think it was God. Why would there be a God
and also a sun? Of course God is the sun.

Everyone in the life before was cranky, I think, because
they just wanted to know.